After the Dragons

This is a work of fiction. All characters, organizations, and events portayed in this novella are either products of the author's imagination or are reproduced as fiction.

After the Dragons

Cover art by Wang Xulin
wangxulin.com

Design by Yu-Lobbenberg, Rachel
racheldesign.myportfolio.com

Edited by Selena Middleton

Published by Stelliform Press
Hamilton, Ontario, Canada
www.stelliform.press

Library and Archives Canada Cataloguing in Publication
Title: After the dragons / Cynthia Zhang.
Names: Zhang, Cynthia, 1994- author.
Identifiers: Canadiana (print) 20210133627 | Canadiana (ebook)
20210133643 | ISBN 9781777091743
(softcover) | ISBN 9781777091750 (ebook)
Classification: LCC PS3626.H36 A78 2021 | DDC 813/.6—dc23

For family, by blood and by choice. For anyone who survived when the world told them they shouldn't.

AFTER THE DRAGONS

CYNTHIA ZHANG

Stelliform Press
Hamilton, Ontario

1

These days, when he is not painting or working, Kai walks and searches for dragons.

They are not hard to find. Not in Beijing, with the water prices still rising and forcing even the rich to curb their luxuries. There have always been strays in Beijing, lurking in the gutters and drifting through crumbling hutong neighborhoods. Now, they also fill the modern quarters of the city: tiny, glittering shapes squirming among lotus-scented suds and tall, wilted calla lilies.

Gingerly, Kai kneels to peer at the jade-green helong flattening itself beneath the dumpster. A thousand or even a hundred years ago, it would have been sacrilege to let a dragon live like this. In the villages near his town, Kai knows that there are many who still worship the dragons, who will row out into the deepest part of the river and drop the first of every harvest into the waters — for the Great Ones, if they should return.

But Beijing is a modern city. There is no time for superstition here, for old gods or sick dragons or hopeless causes. There is only Kai, and he does what he can.

Kai breaks off a piece of sausage, the cheap stuff they sell to kids in little red tubes, then takes a step back. The helong is cautious at first, but hunger soon wins out, and the little dragon is letting him pet it as it licks the grease from the plastic casing. Though the whisker-like tendrils spouting from its muzzle are not quite adult length, the elaborate neck ruff and long horns mark the helong as decidedly male — young and a

3

little skinny, but with a temperament that speaks to an obvious familiarity with humans. He'd be easy to re-home, once Kai got him to the shop.

Looping thin leather jesses around the dragon's back legs, Kai lets the helong settle on one gloved hand and begins the walk home.

On good nights, when the sickness recedes to a perpetual dry throat and the reminder of feverish heat, he thinks, perhaps, that it will be all right. That he can do it, and that this will pass — that it would only be a little while, and he will find himself in Beishida again, the new chalkboards bright and the water clear and no taste of blood when he swallows. That it will be over soon, this bad dream of not enough water and skin that is always too warm, always too dry to touch.

Bad nights —

On bad nights, he knows that there are other ways to do this. That there are alleyways and lean, dark-eyed men; that, poverty grimy and fever-hot as he is, there are still some who would take him — who would take him for it, even. To some, the disease is almost romantic, heroin chic without the track marks, and the thrill of bug chasing without the risk of infection attracts a certain clientele — greasy businessmen with gold buttons and foreigners in expensive suits, come for business and a taste of the local customs. When all else fails, there are tall buildings and reckless drivers, a city of highways and noise and so many ways to disappear.

With the drought, the water prices have risen, and there are days when his illness presses on him. When he longs for before, the luxury of dorm-subsidized water and one-jiao drinks at the water fountain. Water that came cool, prepackaged, showers longer than the five minutes he allows himself each week. And beyond that, buried in a place he does not let himself access, the impossible longing for his childhood bedroom, muffled K-pop filtering from his sister's room and the crackle of frying scallion pancakes from the kitchen —

But there are the dragons, and they must come first.

Mei chirps when he opens the door, flitting over and sinking on his shoulder with sharp claws. She's light, built for speed like all tianlong. But with her long grey wings extended and her neck stretched to rub her face against Kai's, she looms over the helong he's brought home. Understandably startled, the little dragon dives off his fist to scramble under the bed. Kai lets him go; he'll adjust soon enough, and if not, Mei has a talent for bullying friendship out of other dragons. Right now, though, his recalcitrant dragon ignores the newcomer in favor of chattering at him, clicks high and scolding.

"I know, I know," Kai murmurs, one hand reaching to scratch her shoulder blades as he shrugs his backpack off. "I'll feed you soon, all right?"

Now, however, there are other things to do. Tanks to scrub and check, pork bones to clean and make into meal — a thousand small tasks to complete, and always a thousand waiting after those.

The thing they do not tell you about Beijing, Eli realizes three days into his internship with Peking University, is the way people stare.

The other shocks — the toilets, the dryness, the smog — those he had expected, had been prepared for. Had been warned about a dozen times before in brochures and on blogs, by professors and by his mother — *careful about the food*, she had whispered as she hugged him at the terminal, their porter standing awkwardly aside with the luggage, *don't eat anything too greasy or fried. Never drink anything on an empty stomach. Always boil your water first. Try the Peking duck — it is your only chance to have it. Properly, at least. Wear a mask when you're on the train and if you stay out long.* When he had opened his suitcase that first evening in the dorms, he had found a notebook in the top compartment, filled with neat rows of relatives' numbers and cultural landmarks to see.

But what his mother had not mentioned, had forgotten to mention in all her lists and last-minute lectures, had been the stares.

"Wu kuai wu," the woman at the stall says, holding out a cup of soymilk and a length of fragrant, golden dough. Weeks of routine have made theirs a practiced transaction, and now the vendor doesn't even ask for his order when she sees him approaching. Eli hands her a five yuan note and five small coins, nods his thanks, and nibbles at the youtiao as he continues down the street, a dozen pairs of eyes burning on his back.

It isn't their fault, of course. In many ways, China is better than America in this; in China, they see the color of his skin — too dark to be Han Chinese, but light enough to be mistaken for anything from Desi to Middle-Eastern to Latinx — and think *novelty* instead of threat, *curiosity* instead of *criminal*. *American* means bleach-blonde hair and cornflower blue eyes, and while Eli has the clothes and height associated with his nationality, he also has dark skin and curly hair and relative Mandarin fluency. To Beijing residents used to seeing Americans as visiting businessmen and language instructors, these features make Eli even more foreign than his white co-workers, an intellectual puzzle of *but where are you from?* Logically, Eli knows it is an improvement, freakshow instead of horrorshow. And yet there are times, late night walking back from the lab or early mornings on the trains, too little sleep and too much caffeine ringing in his head — there are times, when the pressure of those stares overwhelm him. Hot days and long nights and experiments that never seem to work, his grandmother's ghost on every corner and his mother's questions ringing his ears, *what are you thinking are you crazy what do you think you're doing —*

He thought he'd known once, the answers easy and at the tip of his tongue. It would help his med school application; it would be a chance to conduct cutting-edge research with experts in the field, to connect more fully with a culture he'd known primarily through family vacations and potluck dinners. That was what he had told his mother, the explanations he offered until he wore her resistance down — not completely, of course, because his mother took a lawyer's attitude toward arguments, but enough for her to relent, frowning even as she watched him board the plane.

Eli closes his eyes, the dough suddenly heavy and tasteless in his mouth.

When he opens them, his grandmother is gone, and the city stretches out before him: a palimpsest of old imperial architecture and tall new buildings, narrow streets and wide boulevards and traffic-choked highways that wind together into the shape of Beijing. An abstract expressionist painting of a city, expansive and exasperating by turns, yet somehow familiar despite the disorientation. Somehow right, in a way Eli cannot quite articulate but which he feels in his bones.

As it should be. This is his city, after all, his country even if he does not look the part — his because it had been his mother's city, and before her, his grandmother's city, hers by birth and blood. The city she had been born in, the city she had loved in, the city that — in the end, lungs ashen and hands shaking with fever — she had chosen to die in. Laojia. Home.

In the end, over the doctors and clean air, over the grandson who had just started college, the daughter who had begged her to stay — over all that, his grandmother had chosen to come home.

What are you thinking? Why are you here? What are you doing?

Kai goes to the shop early on Mondays. He does not have to — technically, it is his day off, and as Mr. Lin constantly reminds him, he isn't being paid for it. But he goes anyway, arrives at the steps each morning and sits, waiting, with a sketchbook on his knees. And while Mr. Lin may grumble when he arrives, he always lets Kai in, pulls Kai a seat in the corner as he yells at the new hires.

"No, you moron, we need *four* crates, not two, do you even notice much Tsingtao we sell —"

"Idiot, how long have you been here, can you even remember anything —"

It's a familiar routine. Kai sits there, half-sketching, half-watching as Mr. Lin ignores him and terrorizes the employees. There aren't that many customers in the morning, and with no one watching, Mr. Lin is free to relax all pretense of customer service. The kids cower and stumble at his abuse; their clumsiness only aggravates him more, and before it is noon, Mr. Lin is shoving a rag and a bucket of water at Kai as he glares contemptuously at the newest employee.

Kai does the job quickly and without comment, and when he finishes, Mr. Lin nods and hands him a beer.

They sit for a while, the *whir-whir-whir* of the fan fluttering the edges of the stacked newspapers in the air. In one of the tanks, a small hailong cautiously pads over to his green tank mate who flares his ruff, hissing when the smaller dragon tries to reach the food bowl.

"Juveniles," Mr. Lin says, nodding. "Got them over the weekend, wouldn't shut up all fucking night — you think this is bad, should have seen them this weekend. Thought they'd kill each other by now."

Sipping his beer, Kai watches them. Haunches raised and ruffs fluffed as they circle each other, they look like something out of a classic painting, brought to life in jewel-bright colors.

"They're for the matches?"

"Yeah. Wangzi and Yuqi got sold. Had a void. Had to fill it — so, these fuckers. Hopefully the fighting will wear them out, but who knows. Teenagers, my god. You'll be there?"

8

"Yes." The question is more of a formality than anything at this point. Other than that first shaky weekend, when he had just moved into his new apartment and deactivated his old phone, Kai has not missed the dragon fights.

Mr. Lin nods, short and brisk, then turns back to the store.

"Old man in heaven," he bellows, voice loud enough to make the boy jump and stumble into a nearby post, "what do you *think* you're doing? Did I *say* you could sit there and stare outside? No?"

"You know," Kai says, reaching for a pencil, "maybe if you didn't yell at them so much, they wouldn't make so many mistakes?"

"You don't run this shop, kid."

"Just a suggestion," Kai says, shrugging as he finishes his beer. It's gone flat and, sun-warmed, tastes faintly of paper and dust.

Eli's at the end of his shift, entering data from the week's tests into a spreadsheet when someone knocks on the door. He looks up, expecting to see one of the other interns, Evangeline or Tycho or Jiling, but instead it's his PI standing in the doorway, hands in her pockets as she glances curiously around the lab.

"Dr. Wang," he says, posture automatically straightening as he turns to face her. "Is there something you wanted to talk to me about?"

"Talk about?" Dr. Wang is in her mid-fifties at least but she has a round, open face, the kind more suited to a guileless tourist than one of the world's leading experts on immune-based therapies for chronic conditions. "Oh no, none of that — I'm not here to talk about work, Eli! I was about to leave, but since you're still here, I wanted to ask if you would join me for post-work drinks. My treat, obviously. My friend Lin, he organizes a weekly dragon fight circle, and well, it's a Friday evening, you're here working late — why not take a break and join me?"

For all Dr. Wang's reputation for eccentricity, there's still something strange to Eli about the idea of going out for drinks with his professor. In college, some of his friends had done it, departmental house parties and celebratory post-thesis drinks, but Eli had never had that kind of closeness with any of his teachers.

"Thank you for the offer," he says, "but I shouldn't. I have some work to finish."

"Work? Eli, you're here every morning when I get here, you leave after all the other interns, and when they go out for lunch or drinks, you never go with them. I head this project, so I can justify working late, but you're young and bright and in a new city — you should be exploring and having fun, not spending your nights in the lab. You work too hard."

Eli frowns, caught off guard. "Aren't you supposed to be glad about that?"

"Perhaps," Dr. Wang says, leaning back against the door-frame. "You're my employee, yes, but you're also a future colleague — can't fault me for trying to build connections while I have the chance, can you? I don't know how it is in America, but knowing people is important here, guanxi and all that. Personally, I'm waiting for the day one of my former students cures cancer so I can point at them and say ah-ha, you see? I wrote their recommendation letter to grad school, back when they were still worried if they were smart enough for a PhD program. If you want, you can count it as research. Lin does have some utterly *beautiful* specimens."

"Don't we already have a lab working with dragons?" Eli remembers hearing something about it during the official program orientation, where Dr. Wang had been determined to introduce all her colleagues in the Department of Immunology.

"Dr. Yun's lab has some interesting dragons," Dr. Wang acknowledges, "but it's nowhere near the breed variety Lin works with, and you know how important a diverse gene pool is for proper species-wide research. And the crowd — dragon fighting's a popular sport, so it draws all sorts. Not always the most respectable company, so I hope you won't mention this in front of the administration, but some of them, the things they know! Back when the Europeans came to convert people, they saw our traditional cures, the ginseng and qi charts, and they couldn't understand it, thought it was just superstition and old wives' tales — and yes, a lot of it was that, but look at them now! Studying the antioxidant properties of cinnamon and putting goji berries in every other thing they eat. Which is all to say, Eli," Dr. Wang says, placing a hand on his shoulder, "that curiosity can lead in fascinating directions, and it is occasionally useful to walk off the path of standard procedure."

Eli considers this, Dr. Wang's hand a warm, grounding weight.

"Do I get a choice in this?"

"Not really," Dr. Wang says cheerfully. "It's all right, though. I'll pay."

2

The venue, when they reach it, is a small, faded storefront on a
narrow side street: old houses surrounding either side, roofs
colorful collections of mismatched shingles — not quite hutong
architecture, but still far from the glittering glass and sky-
scrapers of downtown. Newspapers and crumpled
advertisements litter the ground, faded words winking up at
them as they pass.

There's an old man in a rickety chair by the front, a beer in
one hand and a smartphone in the other. He glances up as they
approach, a single, sharp appraisal.

"Wang Jiachun," the man says, standing up.

"Tong," Dr. Wang says, smiling as she steps forward. She
holds out one hand, and they shake. "It seems like it's been
forever since I've been here — work's been ridiculous lately, a
million experiments and PhD candidates all needing committee members, I've hardly been able to breathe. It's been a good
busy, though. Eli," she says, turning to him, "this is Mr. Lin.
He sells dragons and dragon supplies for almost twenty years
now, and he's been helping referee the dragon fights. Tong,
this is Eli, one of the researchers over for the summer program — straight from America. Good kid, but works too hard.
So I said Eli, hey, come on over, have a drink with us, why
don't you? Almost would have said no, too, but I managed to
talk him into it, telling him he could think of it as research. Too
serious, this one," she says, shaking her head. "I thought it was
just our students who were like this, but things are tough in
America too, huh?"

"Hi," Eli says, ignoring his PI's words as he extends a hand. "It's nice to meet you." Mr. Lin's hands are warm and calloused when he shakes, and his grip is strong, the strength of a man distinctly unimpressed by you and unafraid to let you know it.

Dr. Wang's smile practically splits her face as she watches them. Eli is reminded of the house parties his mother would bring him to as a child, and her look of approval whenever he interacted with the other children instead of reading in a corner.

"I was hoping to have a look at that grey-and-white pan-long again — Hua Xue, was it? Quite astonishing, that she managed to survive so long in the city. I would like to examine her more closely. Of course," she says, pulling out her wallet, "the Laboratory of Immunology would be more than happy to cover any costs our demands on your time would warrant."

"If it's a request from Beida's Laboratory of Immunology, well," Mr. Lin says, shrugging as he opens the doors. Dr. Wang walks in beside him, striding forward with the assurance of someone who belongs there. Though not entirely sure why he's needed here, Eli follows, steps slow as he peers inside.

The shop is a dusty, dim space, the only illumination from a single bulb hanging from the ceiling, though unlit lamps are placed throughout the room. While hardly spacious, the shop is larger than it looked from the street, with aquarium tubes stretching up walls like vines and shelves crowded with glass tanks and cages. Dragon scales flash as Eli passes, golden eyes following him with faint curiosity or lazy indifference. There's an astonishing amount of species variation on display — yellow and green and iridescent blue, sizes ranging from the tiny serpents the length of his finger to large wyverns hulking like eagles or brooding vampires inside their metal cages. He pauses in front of one, watching the dragons inside hiss and faintly fluoresce at each other.

"Lin," a voice says. A man emerges from the depths of the shop, dirt streaking his worn apron and scuffed-up sneakers.

He's younger than Mr. Lin, pale and lanky in the way that suggests the delicate mixture of stress and bad nutrition that constitute *college student*. "I need you in the back. I want you to look at —" He stops, seeing Dr. Wang and Eli.

"Oh!" Dr. Wang says, appraising the newcomer in delight. "I haven't seen you around. Did you just start here, young man?"

The young man in question narrows his eyes. Despite being several inches shorter than Eli, his glare is disproportionately withering.

"I've been working here for a month."

"Kai," Mr. Lin says, a warning in his voice before he turns to Dr. Wang again. "Xiang Kaifei. My new assistant. It seems we match now, an apprentice each. Kai, this is Wang Jiachun, medical researcher at Beida."

"Hello," Eli says, inserting himself into the conversation with a wave. "I'm Eli. It's nice to meet you."

"Hi," Kaifei says, glancing at him briefly before turning his attention to Mr. Lin again. "Xiao Bai's refusing to eat again. You should take a look at her."

"Of course she is," Mr. Lin says, sighing as he glances toward the back of the store. "Brat. Didn't I hire you so I wouldn't have to do this? I'll go check on her. Jiachun," he says, nodding at Dr. Wang. "Need to make sure my dragons aren't killing themselves."

"Oh, but I'd love to come along! You know, I was telling Eli about the importance of unexpected experiences — I can't be a hypocrite and refuse now. Besides, it could be helpful later — some of my colleagues at Beida work on dragons, but it's a piecemeal affair since no one does dracology per se. Yueli — you remember Yueli, don't you? She did a postdoc in Shandong, and she's been an evangelist for draconic research ever since. Now she's working with a local wildlife rehabilitation center, but because she's junior faculty the university's been hesitant with funding. I was thinking of petitioning the university to fund a formal dragon research unit, so this visit is

technically research. Who knows, maybe today I'll find something I can add to the grant proposal."

"You do that," Mr. Lin says, expression carefully blank in
the way of someone who has heard this pitch many times
before. "You," he says, nodding at Kaifei. "Watch the front.
Bettors should start coming around in a few minutes — don't
let the place burn."

Kaifei dips his head. "I'll do my best."

"Eli," Dr. Wang says, smiling at him from the back door,
"would you like to come?"

Eli's gaze drifts back to where Kaifei is standing, a stiff
silhouette against the rows of tanks. He shakes his head. "No, I
can wait here."

Dr. Wang gives him an odd look, one full of meaning Eli
can't quite parse, but for once says nothing. With a nod at Eli,
she follows Mr. Lin into a back room, the curtain fluttering
behind them.

In their absence, Eli and Kaifei stand there in the silence.

Eli watches as Kaifei walks behind the register, opening the cabinet and rummaging through its contents with
familiarity.

"So," Kaifei says, not looking up from where he is kneel-
ing, a collection of nets and dried jerky scattered around him.
"You're from Beida?"

"I — yes," he says, blinking. There's a hint of Britishness in
Kai's accent, a not uncommon trait in the English spoken by
international students. "Only here for the summer, though.
Research assistant," he says, switching to Mandarin.

"Mm-hmm. Veterinary medicine?"

"Just normal medicine. Dr. Wang dragged me out here. I
don't really know, either," he says when Kai raises one eyebrow. "She's got these ideas about dragons, thinks that because
of the way their immune and respiratory systems work there
could be a connection to human disease. They could be a
model organism." This last word Eli knows only from hours
spent pouring over lab manuals, Chinese-English dictionary in

15

hand. "I think she feels responsible for me, actually," he says, smiling ruefully. "It's interesting, though. Not a lot of people have dragons in America, so I don't know a lot about them."

"Import taxes, international laws, et cetera." Kaifei pushes the cabinet closed, then stands up. "They're also high-strung, finnicky bastards. If the Western species were half as entitled, you can understand why the Europeans were in such a rush to get rid of them."

Net and bag of food in hand, Kaifei moves toward the back of the store and a row of tanks against the wall. Eli follows, staying a step back as Kaifei adjusts the dials on a tank, flips a switch on another, pops open the top of another and skims dead leaves off the water. The dragon inside — a pale, violently red-eyed shuilong, a river or lake variant Eli guesses by the delicate tracery of veins beneath skin — pokes its head out of the water. A feathery blue mane trails down its spine, and in place of wings, the shuilong has fine, fin-like membranes along its legs to help it navigate through the water. While all shui-long spend a large portion of their lives in water, this dragon looks like it must be a fully aquatic breed, able to breathe above water but receiving most of its oxygen from the long, frilled external gills framing its head.

Sensing human attention, the dragon makes a high, warbling sound, clearly expectant. Kaifei rolls his eyes but acquiesces, sprinkling a handful of pork floss into the tank; it disappears in a matter of seconds, the dragon spraying out the extra water it swallowed.

"Here," he says, shaking a few pieces of dried fish onto Eli's palm and pointing to a small cage near the ground, "you can give this to Suxin. He's not an asshole like some of the others, but be careful where you put your fingers."

Eli blinks. "Thank you," he says, and then leans down, imitating Kai's pose, holding the hand with food just outside the cage. The dragon's tongue is slightly rough against his skin, but not unpleasant. "Are you a student too, then?"

16

"No, not like that," Kaifei says, clicking his tongue as Eli reaches out a hand to pet Suxin. "You don't want to approach them from above, it makes them nervous. Larger dragons sometimes eat the smaller ones, so it's a prey instinct. Like this," he says, extending one hand in front of the dragon, palm up. "Let them smell your hand first, then when he's comfortable, go slow and make sure he can see you when you pet him."

Eli watches, and then tries, as best he can, to mimic Kaifei's movements.

"Is this right?"

"Well," Kaifei says, watching as Suxin leans into his touch, "he hasn't bitten you yet."

"I promise not to hold it against you if he does."

That earns a smile from Kaifei — a small one, but nonetheless it's striking how it transforms his face.

It's oddly calming, sitting there watching as Suxin rubs against his hand. Eli scratches the soft scales underneath Suxin's chin, and the dragon arches its back in response, wings lazily folding and unfolding in pleasure.

Outside, it's getting darker. Small groups of people gather, men in sweat-soaked undershirts lighting cigarettes as they idle in the shade of storefronts. Shoes shuffle; motorcycles groan, headlights fade; someone calls out a name, the sound almost comically loud in the silence. The over-enthusiastic response: an easy embrace by men who would never think to question their heterosexuality.

Kaifei glances toward the doorway, and sighs. "Competitors," he says, standing up. "Should start setting up, the crowds are going to be coming in soon. Tell Lin and your boss to stop canoodling and get over here, will you?"

"C'mon, c'mon, you piece of shit, you little fucker, don't you dare —"

"Oh, fucking gods, I can't *believe* —"

"— no, fuck your mother and fuck your mother's mother and fuck her mother's —"

The courtyard between the shops where Eli and Kai stand is not large. It's a space designated for respite and not activity; crammed with spectators and bettors, it feels even smaller, air thick with the scent of beer and smoke and bodies pressed in uncomfortable proximity. Men crowd the white-chalked circles of the individual rings, screaming vitriol and encouragement by turns. Outside the rings, thin-lipped trainers sit cross-legged and hunched forward, nearly motionless but for the laconic hand motions and whistles which direct their dragons this way or that. Inside the rings, hissing dragons face each other, weighted jesses around their back legs preventing them from flying more than a few meters. Plastic caps have been placed over claws and leather guards cover vulnerable stom-achs and throats. Even with such protections the matches are fierce, the dragons diving at each other and wrestling in the dirt as they try to force their opponent to either step outside the ring or yield in a belly-up surrender. Each time a dragon succeeds, a wave of cheers and groans erupts from the specta-tors. Employees from the surrounding stores circle the crowds, alternatively hawking bottles of beer and smoking as they observe the fights. At one end of the courtyard, opposite the archway through which visitors stream in out of the streets, Mr. Lin sits on a plastic lawn chair, a white T-shirted emperor with his referee whistle and yellow legal pad. Dr. Wang stands beside him, an enthusiastic interloper in her polo shirt and pressed slacks.

"So there it is," Kai says, nodding over his sketchbook at the crowd from where they're standing, close enough so that Kai can nominally monitor the fights while far enough away that they can comfortably talk. "Five thousand years of civiliza-tion."

"Ah," Eli says, uncertain how to respond. Kai's voice is flippant, but his eyes, as they watch the circles of drunk men, are sharp. Eli knows that dragon fighting has a long history in China, a codified emperor's sport more than anything, but he knows that it's always been controversial. Critics compare it to bear baiting and bull fights, other instances of animal suffering for the sake of human entertainment; defenders cite the natural behavior of dragons in the wild and argue that, when correct procedures are followed, the fights provide young dragons a much-needed outlet for otherwise destructive instincts. In lieu of a definitive verdict, the sport is highly regulated, traditional leather armor and claw guards now mandatory, and elaborate new scoring rules have been put in place to minimize injury. But armor slips and plastic breaks and even without evisceration, bruised ribs and broken bones are serious injuries. American-raised and acutely conscious of his country's own history of moral imperialism, its quintessentially American strategy of saving countries by bombing them, Eli tries to avoid casting cultural judgment. There are few things worse to him than being that tourist cliché, the outraged Westerner speaking out against a cultural practice they barely know anything about. But in the face of Kai's obvious outrage, he wonders if there is something hypocritical about the ease with which he brushes away the faint revulsion dragon fighting has always invoked in him.

There's a sketchbook open in front of Kai, but he only glances at it periodically, occasionally erasing a mark here or adding a few tentative lines there. When he tilts his head, they almost coalesce into something, but then Eli blinks and it's gone.

"What are you working on?" Eli asks.

"This?" Kai looks up, face half-shadowed in the artificial light. "It's not — well, it actually isn't anything yet. One of my professors used to talk about feeling in art, the way abstract artists could use a few strokes of line and color to convey emotion. I'm trying that, I guess. Getting down a mood without worrying about representing anything. Being *avant-garde*," he says, the last word accompanied with an eye-roll and heavy French accent.

"*Très bon*," Eli says, shifting so he can better peer at the sketches. "You're an art student, then?"

"Biology," Kai says, idly darkening a few lines in a corner. "Art students don't get paid. It helps with the anatomy, though. You're either chemistry or biology, I'm guessing?"

"Both, actually. Technically just graduated, so I guess I'm not a student anymore either," Eli says, rubbing the back of his neck. "This is sort of like a vacation before I focus on med school applications."

"A vacation where you do research?"

"I didn't want to be completely idle, I guess," Eli says, shrugging. "Might as well try to do something good with all this new free time."

"Eli, Xiao Kai!" Dr. Wang calls. Mr. Lin follows as she approaches. "You two been having a good time, I hope?"

"I'm working," Kai points out, despite the ample evidence to suggest otherwise. Mr. Lin raises a skeptical eyebrow, but Dr. Wang's smile doesn't flag.

"No reason that should stop you from enjoying yourself, though. You boys want anything? A beer, something to eat? I did say I'd pay —"

"We're fine, Dr. Wang," Eli says before she can continue. "How have you two been? Have you been enjoying yourselves?"

"But of course," Dr. Wang says. She links an arm through Mr. Lin's and he adopts the stoic expression of a man resigned to never understanding the ways of extroverts. "Lin da-ge has been showing me all around, and it's quite fascinating. The variety of dragons on display, even within the same species. The level of adaptation in even third or fourth generations, the way cell membranes evolve to maximize water absorption even as the transport proteins become more adept at identifying and filtering out toxins — it makes you wonder if there might be some truth to the rumors, that we might see some trace of huolong —"

Behind his sketchbook, Kai makes a noise of disbelief.

"Oh, come now," Dr. Wang says, pivoting toward Kai, "The basic principle is just evolution, isn't it? Time scale's an issue of course, but look at the peppered moth or pesticide resistance or everything we've done to dogs — nature works faster when humans are involved. If you look at some of the feral populations here, it's the same principle — dragons are supposed to have delicate constitutions, better than canaries for checking air quality. But on any street in Beijing you'll find bright little designer dragons rummaging through dumpsters with their feral cousins. If someone can understand how that happens, locate the mechanisms or genes letting non-native dragons survive high levels of corrosive pollutants, then it's not that far-fetched to think they could use those same principles to bioengineer a dragon that, oh, ingests metals to produce breath that ignites on contact with air. Something sulfuric and maybe iron too — they've certainly found enough ferrous deposits in the fossil record to suggest that's how the old drakes did it. In any case, draconic evolution's a fascinating field, especially when you look at it from the standpoint of model organisms for human health. The implications for respiratory diseases alone ..."

"Of course," Mr. Lin says, voice deadpan. "When you get your patent, I want a portion of the profits. Next round's starting, Jiachun. We should go back. Kai," he says, nodding at him. "Don't start any trouble."

Kai raises a hand in acknowledgement before returning to his sketchbook.

"Huolong?" Eli asks.

"Rumor," Kai says, frowning as he sketches an outline of a building. Eli can make out the edge of a shingled roof, the hazy illumination of streetlamp light. "Pipe dream, urban legend, latest scam since they turned the Water Cube into a theme park. Surprised your boss knows about it. Though considering

21

what I've seen of her, I guess I shouldn't be. Are they all this weird at Beida?"

"I'm just here for the summer," Eli reminds him, "so I wouldn't know. Besides Dr. Wang, I don't interact much with the other researchers. What exactly are huolong, then?"

"It's 'huo' like the huo in 'set fire,' 'forest fire' — fire dragon. It's a rumor you hear around dragon fighting circles sometimes, tales of urban dragons that have adapted to drought conditions by taking on the characteristics of fire drakes, the way animals in Chernobyl are supposed to glow because of the radiation. Beyond blurry internet photos, there's no proof they actually exist, but every now and then, you'll find someone talking about trying to breed back the old European firebreathers. Western dragons, but with Chinese characteristics."

Eli remembers, as a child, going to the Natural History Museum on his visits to London, his father lifting him up for a better view of the *Draco maximus* skeleton on display, each of its teeth as long as his hand. For all that ecologists lament the human-driven extinction of the fire drakes, there is always a hint of relief in their rebukes. Enough stories abound, both apocryphal and not, that it is easy to understand why medieval Europe was so eager to rid itself of the species. *In the West, hidden in the mountains, the dragons grew large and breathed fire and death; in the East, they stayed in the lakes and rivers and spit water, migrations bringing heavy rains and new crops. And so it was that one was hated and feared and the other worshipped and revered.*

"That's rather Jurassic Park, isn't it?"

"A bit." Kai shrugs. "Reviving extinct species is illegal, so it's mostly a bunch of Falun Gong mystics or quacks looking to scam tourists and anyone else stupid enough to fall for it. Once in a while though, you'll get conspiracy theorists and mad scientist types who think that because origin myths say we're supposed to be descendants of the Yellow Dragon, dragon medicine can give us the answer for everything from cancer to aging. Like how drinking tiger bone wine is supposed to make you more virile. Five thousand years of history," Kai says, smiling thinly, "and this is what we have to show for it. All our ancestral animals hunted near extinction or bred into pets."

There's nothing Eli can say to that, so he settles for watching Kai draw. A few feet away, a man prods his dragon back up from the ground, cursing violently as the crowd screams. On the notebook, Kai's fingers tighten.

"Come on," Eli says. Kai glances up, eyes sharp but surprised. "Let's go inside. You said the dragons get restless, right? We should check on them."

It's dark inside the store. A few dragons chirp in protest when Kai flips on the light, but the room is otherwise silent.

Kai glances around the shop, assessing the lines of cages and tanks. Then, without saying a word, he closes the door, slips his sketchpad under the front desk, and walks decisively toward the back of the shop.

After a moment of hesitation, Eli follows. "Do you want any help?" he asks as Kai slips a thick, leather glove over one hand.

"What, and have the whole shop escape? You can stand there, and if I need anything from the top shelves, you can take it down for me."

"I think I can pull that off," Eli says as Kai steps toward a cage in which a blue dragon sits atop a pile of rocks, preening the scales on its back. Compared to the tianlong Eli sometimes sees clustering on rooftops and stop lights, this dragon is larger and sleeker, the size of a hawk with a narrow chest and long curving wings. Feathery frills circle the dragon's head, giving an appearance halfway between a lion's mane and an Elizabethan neck ruff worn by a draconic poet.

Kai makes a high, clicking sound, and the dragon raises its neck toward him, imperious as a little monarch. "Hello to you too, your highness," he says, unhooking the door and sticking his gloved hand inside. The dragon glances at the glove, then back up at Kai: *and?*

Rolling his eyes, Kai takes a dead mouse from one pocket and dangles it in front of the cage. The dragon cocks its head to one side, politely uninterested. "Oh, come on now," Kai says, shaking his hand. "Cixi, baobei, piece of shit, don't be like that —"

"Cixi? Like the empress?"

"Just like the empress," Kai confirms, eyes intent on the dragon as she gingerly steps onto his wrist to take a bite — the smallest bite — of the mouse. "Almost as bad as the human one, too. Bossy little thing," he says, carefully lifting his hand out of the cage, spindly dragon and all. "Isn't that right, princess?"

In response, Cixi trills, licking her snout as she snatches the mouse and swallows it whole. Her eyes are tawny, and in the dim light, they gleam like gold coins against delicate whiskers and blue scales.

"She's beautiful," Eli says, leaning forward. "What is she?"

"A pain in the ass? Careful — this one *does* bite," Kai warns as he hands Eli a strip of dried meat.

Eli offers it to Cixi, who sniffs the jerky before deigning to take it from him.

"In terms of breed, feilong, which goes a long way toward explaining the sense of superiority since they supposedly only appear to 'great men' in the wild." Kai strokes her neck, Cixi leaning into the touch before snapping at his fingers. "Doesn't do anything to explain the stubbornness or complete lack of manners."

"Like owner, like dragon, maybe?"

Kai glances up, and for a second, Eli is unsure whether he's earned the right to say what he did — but then Kai laughs, a short, surprised sound that turns into a wry smile. Eli can't help smiling back. And then, with no warning whatsoever, Cixi swoops off Kai's wrist and out the door, a glistening blue blur with Eli's jerky between her teeth.

"Oh, fuck," Kai mutters before sprinting after her.

Eli takes longer to recover, and then he's racing after Kai and the escaped dragon.

Cixi doesn't go far — a few streets away, where the old buildings abruptly break into an abandoned park. Flattened soda cans and worn plastic bags litter the grass, the few trees skinny and newly planted, but it must be naturalistic enough for Cixi, who is perched on the highest branch of the tallest tree.

They approach her slowly, Eli trying not to breathe too heavily. It hadn't been a long chase, but he's spent the majority of the last four years in labs and lecture halls.

Kai is comparatively unruffled. "You're taller," he says. "You could try to climb up."

Eli scans the tree in all its slender height. Up close, the tree is both thinner and taller than it had looked from afar. "I'm pretty sure I'd break it."

"True," Kai concedes. He frowns, watching Cixi preen herself. Reaching in his pocket, he takes out another strip of jerky, holding it between two fingers in front of him. "Come on," Kai says, whistling as he dangles the meat in the air. In the tree, Cixi cocks her head, seems to consider the merits of descending. "Come on, you little shit, I don't have time for this —"

Her angle, as Cixi lands, is a little awkward, more a falling missive than a graceful plane; as Kai stumbles under her weight, Eli — before he can think — steps forward, one hand grabbing Kai's arm to steady him.

"Thank you," Kai says, nodding as he briskly shakes off Eli's grip. "It would have been fine, it happens all the time, but still —"

But Eli is frowning at his hand as if it had been burnt.

"Hey," he says, "are you okay? You're warm — I think you might have a fever or —"

25

Kai stiffens and Eli realizes several things at once. The dryness of his skin. The warmth, vivid as an August afternoon. And in the low light, the flush in his face — had it always been that red? Had he just not noticed? — the spots of red, like bloody freckles on pale skin —

Kai's eyes widen, the faintest, briefest hint of anger showing through the shock. And then he turns, quiet as a shadow, and walks away.

Eli can't move. He's unable to talk, a montage of images swirling through his mind: blackened lung tissues and the sharp sunken faces of stage four patients, the rows of medications that had lined his grandmother's counter in video calls. Eli's not stupid, he knows it's unlikely, that there are a dozen other reasons for what he's seen, what he *thinks* he's seen —

He's worked with it in the hospitals before, seen dozens of second and third-stage patients flown over from Beijing and Delhi, and he knows this, is as familiar with this disease as if the symptoms were written on his own skin —

Shaolong. Throat scorch. Caused by long exposure to poor air quality, especially common in cities with high pollution indexes and poor environmental regulations —

The same disease that killed his grandmother.

There was a time, immediately after diagnosis, when Kai thought about killing himself.

After the months of coughing, the weeks of concerned teachers asking if he was all right, when he finally sat down in the doctor's office, he had heard the words as if from far away — shaolong. Two characters, so often heard and said, and yet for all that, distant. Not here but somewhere else.

Always odd, Kai thinks, when it happens to you. Before, reading about it in papers, seeing it on television — and then

26

one day, without warning, you're living that reality. His own name another series of pixels in the array of images comprising a death sentence. Shaolong: burnt lung. First documented case appearing in the 1990s, initially mistaken for emphysema before a doctor at Beida noticed the distinct patterns of tissue corrosion that would come to be the disease's signature prognostic. Affecting a small percentage of urban dwellers, typically the old and sickly.

Kai had never thought of himself as sickly. Not before. He'd been careful — followed all the health clinic pamphlet tips about using condoms and testing regularly, didn't smoke or do drugs or leave his drinks unattended at bars. He'd been good, he thought. He should have been safe. He couldn't have known that the danger would be in the air around him, every breath another inhale of slow poison worse than anything his roommates had ever smuggled into the dorms.

After the doctors had finished rattling off their diagnosis — *stage two though we'll need more tests to determine a full treatment regime. Please make a follow-up appointment at the front desk* — he had walked out of the clinic. Brushed off the nurses without hearing their queries, their *"who are you looking for where are you going do you need help?"* passing off him as though not they were not there.

He doesn't remember much of what happened after that. Only that his surroundings seemed suddenly comprised of too many colors, shining sickly like an oil slick or water running off loose scales. Somewhere, sometime, he thinks someone had called him; somewhere, sometime, he thinks he'd ignored them. Let his phone ring and ring, paying it as much mind as he did the street vendors with their paper-clip structures and paper games.

Somehow, he'd found himself in Chaoyang, wandering the Olympic Green and the shadows of empty, indeterminate stadiums; somehow, he'd found himself on top of one, metal creaking beneath him as he clamored his way onto the edges of the roof overhanging the stands. In the distance, the Bird's

Nest loomed, a marvel of elegantly woven metal even after all those years. Kai had been too young to care much when the Summer Olympics happened, but he had heard his parents talk about it: the broadcasts full of fireworks and smiles, the child singers and performers from all the four corners of China. The million hazy faces of the foreign tourists, teeth white and hair golden in the click-click-click of camera flash light. He wondered what it must have been like then, paint still bright and now-empty stands full of millions. All that money and effort, whole neighborhoods torn down to make room for a new and brighter China — would it have been worth it, to be here for that one blaze of international glory?

He looked down. A few streets over, groups of late-night pedestrians cluster around the glow of street lamps and late night mini-marts. Directly below, though, there is nothing but empty sidewalks and once brightly painted sculptures, now mere blurry shapes from Kai's current height. What it would be like to fall, to throw himself off? How would his body look when it hit the ground? Red flesh bursting open like a too-ripe persimmon. Would it still be identifiable after that? He supposed it would be — there would be enough blood, enough fingerprints and peeling skin to find out who this corpse had once been. Would they care enough to do that for him, some dusty dropout with death in his lungs?

He remembered thinking that, faintly comforted in the idea that at least his mother would never know. He remembered standing there, at the top of the stadium, for a very long time.

It had been a Saturday night. No one would have noticed his disappearance.

And then the dragons had come — one, two, a whole unlikely flock of tianlong, chattering in rapid dragon-speak as they flew around him. Green and brown and copper and a few rare darts of import blue — the largest of them barely the size of swallows, but as fierce as their larger ancestors and braver and more boisterous than any bird. A few, seeing him there, puffed out their chests at him, bared fangs as thin as needles; others, curious by this newcomer in their midst, perched on his shoulders, his jacket, the top of his head. A few nipped curiously at his hands; one or two stuck thin tongues inside his jacket. One licked at a cut on his hand from climbing up, the blood already dry. Its tongue was cool and wet against his skin.

It lasted a minute, two minutes — tianlong were fickle creatures, the small ones even more so — and then they were gone, curiosity sated as they blew away with the breeze. Leaving him standing there, alone, feeling much lighter for the missing weight of thirty small bodies.

Below him, the cool Beijing night and its inhabitants passed by — young mothers in high heels, green-haired boys defying death with cigarettes and skateboards, giggly schoolgirls wearing uniforms and their mothers' lipstick. From up here, they were no more than pinpoints of pink, the outline of girls in cell phone light, but he knew how their faces would look up close, done-up and thin in the pale streetlight. The cloying sweetness of perfume hanging on their clothes, the way their laughter would sound, young and shrill and catching.

He stood looking over it all.

And then, carefully, he climbed back down.

Dr. Wang invites the lab to dinner a week later and, try as he might, Eli can find no way of getting out of it.

They end up in a private room on the fifth floor of a hotel, each plate setting laden with three plates and three glasses — water, wine, and delicate glasses for the deadly bottle of Maotai several of the international researchers had brought. Dr. Wang orders hot shaobing and Peking duck and jellied liangfen swimming in chili oil and vinegar, piling food onto the plates of the students within reach and scowling at the rest until they fill their plates as well.

It's awkward at first, language barriers and the inherent difficulty of the Beida/exchange student split, but the wine and the Maotai soon make themselves felt. Waitresses drift in periodically, and they find increasing inventive ways to make room on the table for steaming tureens of five-spice fish and dandan noodles. Tycho flirts with an undergraduate; Evangeline and Jiling, having made their way through most of the bottle of red wine they'd brought, are rapt as Dr. Yun — twenty-eight, witty, already an assistant professor and the subject of much student attention — describes her encounter with the novelist Mo Yan at Shandong University, long hands cutting patterns through the air as she speaks. At the head of the table, Dr. Wang shines her bright smile over the scene, a monarch ensconced among her self-chosen court.

Eli, sensing that the serious toasting is about to begin, excuses himself to the bathroom. He closes the door behind him, careful to muffle the sound of his exit, before walking toward the floor's back balcony.

It's hot outside, but after the aggressive air conditioning of the restaurant, it's a pleasant heat. A few waitresses glance at him as they pass between tables and banquet rooms, but they otherwise let him be, no doubt used to the vagaries of foreigners and customers alike.

Eli leans against the rail and closes his eyes.

"There you are," someone says from behind him. Eli turns, and Dr. Wang is there, a pack of cigarettes held loosely in one hand.

"Wang laoshi," he says, straightening. "Is there something you wanted?"

"Something I want? Nothing more than the pleasure of your company. I know I'm your employer, but I do try to keep a basic interest in my researchers' lives. The movies might love lone geniuses tinkering away in their labs, but most of us prefer a little more company than that." She smiles, friendly and unassuming, an expression that makes it easy to forget her numerous scientific awards as well as her status as Eli's boss. "You've been acting odd lately. Is something wrong, Eli?"

"I'm sorry?"

"Oh, come on, now," Dr. Wang says, tutting. "You're in a foreign country, you're far from your friends, you don't know anyone, and people stare at you in the street. How are you doing?" Dr. Wang proffers a cigarette; when Eli shakes his head, she nods. "Good. Ruins your lungs, smoking. My daughter calls it 'the slowest form of premeditated suicide.' But when everyone else does ..." She shrugs, rueful.

"If everyone jumps off a cliff," Eli says, moving to make room at the balustrade.

"True," Dr. Wang admits, "but what sort of life would that be, without friendship? *A life with integrity*, Lanlan would say, but that's why she works in nonprofits and I don't. Now," she says, taking a spot next to him and lighting her cigarette, "tell me, how are you settling into Beijing?"

"I'm fine," Eli says, shrugging as he evades Dr. Wang's eyes. "I mean, there's been a bit of an adjustment at times, having to find alternatives to Google and other websites I'd usually use, but it's fine. I can handle it."

"Then what is it? Is it everything all right at home? Is it a girl? I'll admit, I would expect that more from Tycho than you, but I suppose one can never truly predict young love —"

"What? No, of course not, it's nothing like that, why would you think — it's not that," Eli says, sighing. Below them, the pedestrians mill, mothers carefully guiding their children past bright storefronts and the clusters of chatting teenagers gathered in front of them. "It's the boy from the store. Mr. Lin's assistant."

"That young man? Kaifei, I think he said his name was?"

Eli nods. "Xiang Kaifei. I was talking with him, and I think, or I thought I saw — he's sick. Shaolong."

Dr. Wang leans against the balcony, taking a drag on her cigarette. "And?"

Eli stares at her.

"Yes," Dr. Wang says, staring out toward the city lights, "I knew. Don't look so surprised. I've done enough clinical work to see the signs. He hides them well, but they're still there. If you know how to look."

"Then why didn't you say something? He — that's not right, he should be in a hospital. He should be getting help — there are free trials at Beida, we could have offered him a place —"

"Do you think he would have accepted it?"

Eli thinks of his grandmother, sipping tea and petting one of her innumerable cats as she told them the news over video chat. The terrible calm with which she preemptively answered his mother's protests, telling her no, she would not be returning to the States to receive further care.

"But," he says. "We have to do something. We need to — he needs help."

"Perhaps he has his own reasons for not wanting help. Shaolong is a terminal disease, Eli. Perhaps not forever, maybe not even for long, but certainly for now. Yes, technically patients with stage one can live an almost ordinary life if it's caught then, but it rarely is. By the time patients come in complaining about chronic coughing or shortness of breath, they're nearly always at stage two at least, and disease progression accelerates from there. Even before oxygen masks and ventilators become necessary for sufficient airflow, patients know that treatment is less about a cure than slowing the symptoms. The question isn't *if* but *when* and in how much pain."

"Is that what you tell all your patients?"

"No," Dr. Wang says. "But it's what you tell yourself, afterwards."

The flashing signs of the phone stores and the street vendors blend together far below them and Eli and Dr. Wang watch the sharp cacophony of light. Actual sound floats up slowly, a distant soundtrack not quite real.

32

"He needs help, though," Eli says, staring at the figures below. "It's not too bad yet, but it'll only get worse. He knows that. He has to know that."

"Maybe he does. Some people, though," Dr. Wang says, "they'd rather not get help. They find it shameful, or they have families they need to support, or they would simply rather not spend a large portion of their remaining lives hospital bound. Retain some face in their last few years. You hear it from the older patients sometimes, the ones whose children bring them in. It's hard, then, deciding what to do."

"And what do you do then?"

"The best I can," Dr. Wang says, tapping her cigarette against the railing. "That's all you can do in the end."

In the daylight, unaccompanied by Dr. Wang, the shop is smaller than Eli remembers it, shabbiness cast into full relief. The tanks, luminescent in the darkness, are older in the light of day, glass scratched up and foggy with old water stains.

When Eli steps inside, Kai is sitting cross-legged at the back of the shop, sketchpad open on his knees. He doesn't immediately look up, but soon he notices Eli lingering by the doorway, hands behind his back as he studies a shelf of brightly colored pet toys.

"Hello," Eli says.

Kai takes time to stand. "Hello," he says, collecting his sketchpad under one arm — Eli catches a glimpse of blue wings and the edge of a building on the half-hidden paper. "I didn't expect you here."

Eli shrugs. "I had fun when I was here before. I wanted to visit again."

"Ah."

Eli nods. The silence between them is palpable, awkwardness hanging in the air like smog in the sky.

"If you're here to pity me," Kai says, "please let me know now, so I can leave."

It's said in such a casual, calm tone, no flicker of emotion passing over his face as Kai politely meets his gaze. Eli wonders how Kai would have reacted if he'd gone the way he had originally wanted to, offered the idea of a clinical study or financial help, and is glad that Dr. Wang had persuaded him against it.

"No," he says. "I have an offer for you."

"An offer?"

Eli nods. "Dr. Wang — when we came the other night, she was talking about starting a new program, one for studying draconic evolution and applying the results to human respiratory research. The department has a few dragons right now, as part of a collaboration with the Beijing Wildlife Rescue and Rehabilitation Center. Yun Yueli leads that project, but Dr. Wang used to be her mentor, so there's a lot of student overlap between their labs. Dr. Yun's focus is regenerative medicine, not dracology, and while the immunology department's done a lot of poaching from zoology and vet med students, they don't have anyone who specializes in dragons. If you're willing to come in as a student employee, Dr. Wang and Dr. Yun said there's room in the departmental budget. It wouldn't be much — an hour once or twice a week, to check in and make sure that we're doing everything right. You'd be paid for it, of course."

"Would I, now?"

"One hundred RMB for each visit."

Kai raises an eyebrow. "That's a lot of money for what I'd be doing."

"It'd be less than paying an expert to come in."

"Cheap labor. Ingenious."

"Something like that," Eli agrees.

Kai is somewhere far away, lost in a contemplation where Eli cannot follow. "Your professor's lab," he says finally. "What supplies does it have for the dragons?"

"The usual, I guess," Eli says, blinking. "Medicine, sedatives, food, different stuff depending on the age and requirements of the dragon ... Why?"

"Do they need all of it?"

"The dragons come in and out on a rotating basis, but from what Dr. Wang's said, they don't seem strapped for supplies. Why?"

"I won't take the money," Kai says, "but I'll take the supplies."

Eli wants to ask what an ill college student would want with bags of grain-free pet food, but Dr. Wang's words echo in his mind and he nods.

"All right," he says. "It's a deal, then. What day would you want to start?"

"Sunday's fine," Kai says, already turning back to his sketchpad. "Give me your number, and we can work it out from there."

3

The water prices are rising.

Drought has barely touched the richer neighborhoods, the fountains at foreign nightclubs still running and the flowers lush as ever on university lawns, but it is noticeable, nonetheless. In the hutongs and poorer neighborhoods, shirtless children streak down the streets, their mothers chasing after them in little more than their modest underwear, bra straps visible through thin undershirts. In many ways, it is more an economic issue than an environmental one, taxes for water and electricity curbing air conditioning for those who could afford it. But that does not make it any less real. Not for the grandparents hospitalized from heatstroke, the homeless amputees crouched in shopping malls for relief, the harried mothers with nothing but lullabies to soothe their crying children.

And with the rise in prices, of course, come more dragons.

In his apartment, window open to circulate air, Kai sits on a chair a few feet away from the kitchen table, staring at the open wire cage with the dragon crouching inside.

He reaches for the syringe and canister of morphine next to him. In the cage, the feilong shifts, hackles rising as its eyes follow him, but Kai ignores it. It's been four hours since he first lured the dragon out from the boarded-up shell of what was once a liquor store, and if it still hasn't forgiven him for tricking it with fresh tilapia, there's little sense in waiting longer.

Kai pulls on his gloves — the worn pair he'd appropriated from a Beida supply closet — and stands up. Backed against one side of the metal cage, the feilong tenses, tendrils flattening against its head as it eyes him. For all the fury and grime, it's a beautiful creature: long, proud neck and wide wings stretched nearly translucent at the top, scales a jade green rarely seen outside of captivity or Photoshop. Kai can't imagine how much its owner must have spent on it; or why, having spent that money, they would unceremoniously throw the creature out. Beijing's rich and sophisticated may hold little with folk tradition, but Kai had thought even they would balk at abandoning a creature traditionally associated with luck.

The dragon shifts, crouched low as it hisses, teeth bared and spittle dripping down its chin. Ribs showing and one wing bent and streaked with blood, it looks nothing like a symbol of fortune and wealth. Right now, this feilong is just a hurt and frightened animal.

In her cage, Mei chirps anxiously, wings shuffling together as she repositions herself on her perch. The other dragons are quiet, observing the drama instead of participating. Mei is friendly with new dragons, but she makes clear that Kai is her human. He has no doubt that if he let her roam free as he tended to the feilong, Mei would flare her ruff and hiss in a display that would best anything the weakened feilong could muster.

"Easy," he says, approaching the table where the cage sits, top open and a spitting dragon inside. "Shh, it's all right, just let me have a look —"

He lunges forward, stabbing the needle into one green flank; the dragon, just as swift, swipes claws down the length of his arm. Mei screeches, wings flapping against the bars of her cage, but Kai ignores her, focusing on pushing the plunger of the syringe down.

As soon as he finishes, Kai drops the syringe, hissing as he pulls away, clutching his arm to his chest. The scratches aren't deep, or even particularly long, but they will need to be

37

dressed before he continues — too high a risk of bacterial contamination, and he can't afford that, not with his immune system overworked as it is. Grating as it is to remember, his body isn't an inconvenience he can ignore anymore, not when shaolong means even minor injuries can spiral into feverish agony. A former adherent of mind over matter, Kai resents this new awareness of his body. But as with so many other recent changes, there is nothing to do but live with it.

"I should have stolen some chloroform, too," Kai tells the feilong as he bandages his arm. In response, the creature leans back on its haunches and hisses at him. From her cage, Mei hisses back, baring her teeth as she glares at the other dragon, pupils narrowed to black slits against gold irises. "Oh, hush," Kai tells her, "I'm fine." Melodramatic, all of them. Melodramatic and overprotective.

He'll have to get sedatives, Kai thinks as he takes the first aid kit from under his bed, the next time he visits Beida. Not chloroform, perhaps, but tranquilizers at least, if they have them. If not — well, he's managed so far without them.

Eli would find some way to get the supplies to him if he mentions it, Kai knows. Buying him lunches and bottled water, pretending he isn't staring when he thinks Kai won't notice ... it would be sweet, the way he hovers, if Kai didn't know Eli was watching him for signs of weakness.

Kindness, he thinks as he presses the last bandage down. Objectively worry is not a negative quality; the presence of concern speaks positive things about Eli and his capacity for compassion. But Kai has never been good at accepting other people's pity, kindness or not. Not when he was ten, standing under the summer sun in new shoes and a scratchy suit as he watched black-suited men lower his father into the ground, distant aunts whispering *oh, how terrible, that poor woman, and those poor children* ... Not when he was fifteen, the provincial scholarship kid at his elite city high school, orientation not technically public but the knowledge of it present in everything he did, another barrier between him and his rich classmates. Certainly not now, twenty-one and living alone in an apartment for which none of his friends know the address, his phone number strategically changed and all social media deleted. Old life carefully compartmentalized and put away.

Next to the cage, his mother's latest letter sits, poached from his old dorm address. It's unopened — Kai knows what it will say. *Hello Kai Kai; how are you doing? How is the city? Xiao Xue is doing well in class. You don't have to send money home; have fun! Don't work too hard. Don't go to bed too late and don't forget to eat breakfast — I know you're busy, but you're not too busy for a few bites of congee. Let us know if you ever want to visit home, okay? We miss you.*

Kai knows it's cowardice, not letting them know, but he can't stand the idea of seeing the change in his mother's and sister's faces.

Turning away, Kai sits down opposite the table again. The feilong crouches back in response, hisses at him — still hostile, but slower, less focused. The morphine is beginning to work, no doubt, and thank god for that; it's nearly noon and Kai doesn't have the luxury of hours to spend on a single stubborn dragon.

Sedatives next time, though. Oral, if he could find them. Sedatives and arm guards, if he can find them.

Eli calls his mother on Monday, the way he has every week since arriving in Beijing. Sitting on his dorm bed, he waits for the WeChat connection to stabilize, but then his mother is there, blinking at the phone camera.

"Hi Mom," he says, smiling as he leans back against the bedframe.

"Hi to you too, Eli." On the screen, his mother's face is small, blurred as she shuffles back on their old couch. "How have you been?"

"Good. Busy, but I've been good. How have you been?"

"Completely bored, now that you're gone. Your dad suggested I get a dog. One of those hypoallergenic ones, a Shih Tzu or poodle or doodle-whatever. I think I might actually do it."

"As long as you let me name it," Eli says, smiling. His father lives in London now and has since remarried, but his parents remain one of the most amicably divorced couples he knows. It was hard on all of them in the beginning, but Eli suspects, sometimes, that the divorce had meant more to him than it had to them. As academics, perhaps they had been better at rationalizing the reasons for their split — differing goals, homesickness, his father's self-admitted tendency for throwing himself into research at the expense of meals and soccer practices and bedtime stories. Seven at the time, Eli had only known that his father was gone. Now Eli can better understand his father's anxieties over fatherhood and life in a country with no other family close by, but that seven-year-old's hurt lingers, somewhere deep and immovable.

"How's the science?" his mother asks. "Discovered any cures for cancer lately?"

"It's been sciencey," he tells her. For all her brilliance in other areas, his mother is a bit of a liberal arts cliché when it comes to his research: she knows that Dr. Wang does medicine and that his current research focuses on respiratory illnesses, and that is the self-admitted limit of her interest in specifics. "Curing cancer is still a work-in-progress, but I'm learning a lot. Dr. Wang took the lab out to dinner the other night and ordered a ridiculous amount of food, so I don't think I'll have to cook for a while."

"Fancy," she says, smiling. "And the other students? Making any friends?"

Eli isn't sure how to answer that. It's been a few weeks since Kai started showing up at the lab to check over Dr. Yun's dragons, and Eli still can't help being a little surprised each time he does. Even as Kai recommends changes in feeding and exercise schedules ("just because they don't need to hunt for their food here doesn't mean they should stay in their cages all day"), there's still a feeling of transience to their meetings. Friendship requires voluntary enjoyment of each other's company, and Eli can't shake the sense that Kai, with his curt words and careful neutrality, is merely humoring him.

"More or less," Eli says instead. "Everyone's nice, and we get along. But we've only known each other for a few months. We're more coworkers than anything, so it's hard to say exactly. I told you Mom, we don't have that much in common. They're much more about the alcohol and girls, and I'm ... not."

"And thank God for that," his mother says, so empathetically that Eli laughs. "Still, you should still go sometimes. Have fun. I won't tell your father so long as you keep safe. And who knows, you could be a good influence on them, maybe."

"Babysit them, you mean?" Eli smiles, picking at a loose thread on his bedspread. "Somehow, I don't think being designated killjoy is going to improve my popularity much."

"Oh, I don't know," his mother says, smiling. "You're responsible, baobei; people tend to appreciate that, even when they won't admit it."

Eli isn't sure he agrees, but he lets it go. *Responsible* is an odd word, a descriptor that's been applied to him ever since he was a chubby-cheeked seven-year-old offering to help teachers clean up after art class. A good student, the responsible friend, de facto group project leader and designated driver — people have always offered these assessments with a faint tinge of awe, as though Eli is somehow exceptional for keeping appointments and doing what he said he would. Eli, for his part, never understood it. Someone had to wash the dishes and make sure there was Tylenol and coffee for post-party

41

hangovers. If none of his friends were up to the task, why was it remarkable that Eli would volunteer?

"You know," Dr. Wang had said when Eli first told her about his offer to Kai, "you're going to have to be careful." It'd been such an incongruous response, the exact opposite of what a normal reaction to learning your employee had promised unlimited laboratory supplies to a total stranger, that at first Eli didn't know what to say. Dr. Wang had smiled, her look sympathetic yet somehow bittersweet as she cupped her hands around a mug of tea. "You want to help, yes, and that's understandable and laudable, but you have to remember that you can't do everything. You can give him options, yes, but you can't make him decide. He isn't your responsibility."

But if not mine, Eli remembers thinking, *then whose?*

"How's the weather?" his mother asks, the change in topic so abrupt Eli can tell it is what she has been waiting to ask all along.

"Hot," he says, shrugging. "Dry. Same as always. I'm wearing my mask, and the coordinators have trips out of the city every other weekend, so it's all right, Mom. The news exaggerates."

"Hmm," his mother says, noncommittal. It's an old argument: she had never liked the idea of him going to Beijing in the first place, had refused to answer his calls for a month after he told her. Yet as much as the silence had hurt, a reminder of the silences that had permeated the house after first his father left and then his grandmother refused to return, Eli could not blame her for it.

His grandmother, before she died, had asked to be buried in Beijing. The suddenness of her death meant there had no time to renew expired visas, so that while Eli sat the MCAT, his mother watched distant cousins lower his grandmother into the ground.

"Mom," he says, trying his best to project reassurance with his words and smile. "It's all right. Everyone's nice, and I'm having a good time, so you don't have to worry, okay? We're going to visit Jingshan Park next weekend. It'll be a day trip and everything."

"Jingshan is still in the middle of the city. Not that much a change of scenery when you get technical about it."

"*Mom.*"

"You can choose to not listen to me, but you can't stop me from worrying, Eli. That's my right as your mother."

"You don't need to worry about this, though. I swear, Mom, I'm fine. Honestly."

His mother frowns, lips pursed and unhappy, but she lets it go.

"Do you need anything?" she asks. "If you need more money for food or souvenirs or anything from home, we can always transfer money into your account ... it might take a while, but we can send it over if you need it."

"I'm fine," he says, smiling as reassuringly as he can. "Thanks for offering though."

"Take care of yourself, baobei," she says, and then she's gone too.

Despite how frequently he visits Mr. Lin's store, it's a few weeks after he starts working with Kai that Eli attends another dragon fight.

It is, in the end, less a deliberate moral choice than one of convenience — for all that Eli finds the sport unpleasant, he isn't Kai, ready to strike some grand ethical stance at the slightest injustice. In college, his friends had teased him about being secretly middle-aged, and though he'd protested, Eli knows that it's at least partially true; he's never liked parties or festivals, the constellations of noise and lights and drunken cheer exhausting after a few minutes. The fights Mr. Lin referees are hardly on the scale of the music festivals and frat parties Eli's housemates had dragged him to, but it's the same principle: too many people, too much noise, not enough space to think. But Dr. Wang had invited him and he'd vowed to make the best of it. Nursing a beer on the outskirts of the ring, watching men cheer on their favorites, Eli wonders, once again, what exactly is the appeal of these fights.

"You look like you have a question," Dr. Wang says.

Eli deliberates over his words, then settles on honesty. "I don't understand why we're here again."

"Because it's a learning opportunity," Dr. Wang says. "Also, if I'm going to let a stranger into my laboratory to rummage through my equipment, I'd prefer to know a little about them first." Her tone is light, but Eli can't help but wince at the unspoken implications. For all her friendliness, Dr. Wang is still his PI, letting Kai help as a favor to Eli.

"Besides," Dr. Wang says, one shoulder rising in a shrug, "it's nice to get out of the lab sometimes, isn't it? Engage with people once in a while, see where all the work you do is actually going. There's value to studying phenomena directly, seeing the way principles actually work in the world instead of under controlled and artificial conditions. A learning experience, like I said. The process is messier, yes, but sometimes science is like that. Stumbling in the dark until we reach something of value. And when we do, who are we to complain about the discovery not being what we expected?"

She smiles at Eli, earnest and friendly, and in the face of that expression, Eli cannot find it in himself to respond. He remembers feeling that way about research once, and he cannot imagine how Dr. Wang, with all her years of experience, has managed to maintain it.

"Ah, Tong, just in time," Dr. Wang says, smiling as Mr. Lin walks over with an unlit cigarette. "That man over there, with the green panlong? I had a few questions about its foreclaws, the extra dewclaw there, and well, he doesn't seem to know much. I was wondering if I could ask you a few questions —"

The animation on Dr. Wang's face as she turns to Mr. Lin tells Eli that he's on his own for the next few hours. There's nothing to do, then, but find Kai where he is perched on a stool with a sketchpad balanced on his knees.

"Hi," Kai says, glancing up. "I thought I saw your professor around."

"You don't sound particularly happy about it."

"I'm not," Kai says, turning back to his drawing. "She's nosy and tactless and asks a thousand questions no one cares about or could even answer, and she doesn't seem capable of talking to people under fifty like they aren't middle schoolers." He frowns, turning his pencil on the side and shading upwards in slow, steady strokes.

"That's a fairly accurate description," Eli says, "if not exactly charitable." He leans in for a closer look at the paper. "What are you working on?"

In response, Kai tilts his sketchbook toward him. It's a dragon — Cixi, Eli guesses from the long lines of wings and thin limbs, though it could plausibly be another feilong. The expression of distant superiority, however, is pure Cixi, the likeness striking even with the sketch in black-and-white and only half-finished. Eli can see the thrumming energy in the creature's folded wings, the gloss of its scales.

"That's very good."

"Says the one who's never drawn before."

"What? Does that mean I can't have an opinion?"

"Essentially, yes."

"I've drawn before," Eli protests. "Not in a formal context — but I have artsy friends, I've been to museums. I like to think I know a bit about the process. I still think it's good."

Kai makes a noncommittal noise, but otherwise lets the point stand.

Compared to the first fight, there are only a smattering of people this time. Kai had told Eli that attendance dies down after the opening fights, with fans waiting to see which dragons pull ahead in wins. Eli guesses that tonight's attendees are diehards and novice trainers looking to pick up hands-on insight; at a glance, Eli sees several notebooks and at least one laptop opened to a spreadsheet. Without the need to please a raucous crowd, individual fights are shorter, dragons pinning or knocking their opponents out of bounds with swift, economical moves. In front of a shuttered storefront, Dr. Wang gestures wildly with her hands, no doubt expostulating on some advanced scientific theory as Mr. Lin watches. It's difficult to tell from this distance, but Eli thinks Mr. Lin is smiling.

"It's a slow night," he says, turning to Kai. "Do you want to go somewhere else for a while?"

"Please," Kai says, already standing up.

When Eli takes in his surroundings, they're far enough from the shop that he knows he wouldn't be able to pick his way back by himself. But they're close enough that he doesn't doubt Kai will be able to. In any case, Kai is relaxed and assured, leading them — along with Cixi and a small dragon he'd fetched from the shop — through the narrow streets. He punches in the key code for the gated apartment complex with practiced ease.

Eli passes through the gate as Kai pacifies the dragon on his right shoulder. Tianlong instead of feilong, the dragon is smaller than Cixi and far less self-assured. Perched on Kai's forearm, Cixi gives an impatient trill, obviously unimpressed with her companion's skittishness.

"Do you live here?" Eli asks, glancing around. The presence of a gate is already unexpected, and the buildings inside the compound are tall and white-washed, clean in a way that suggests either constant maintenance or newness. Small patches of vegetation line the space between buildings, impressively green despite the current weather. It's certainly fancier than any place he would expect a college student to live.

"No," Kai says, holding tight to the leather straps around Cixi's legs as he closes the door behind them. "Barely anyone lives here — they finished construction a year ago, but since then, no one's really moved in. They're trying to create a new luxury housing and hotel district, but the rest of the neighborhood's preventing that from happening. Even if the buildings are nice, most rich people would rather move to the suburbs than live someplace so 'unsafe.' It's a local joke, all these deserted high-rise buildings with their fancy car garages in an area where no one owns a car."

"How did you know the code, then?"

"Observation," Kai says, turning back and giving him a smile. And for an instant, his smile is so self-satisfied that he could be any other college student, basking in the victory of breaking the rules.

On Kai's arm, Cixi strains upwards as they walk, trying to escape. But Kai keeps a tight hold on her jesses. On his shoulder, the other dragon — Qinglu, brown-red and smaller — watches her, blinking in the draconic equivalent of wide-eyed gawking.

Kai stops in an expanse of sparse half-dried grass. The remnants of a playground litter the space — a set of swings bordered by a red seesaw and two cartoon characters on spring-loaded mounts — but for the most part, the area is empty save for the occasional sapling. How much would this space have cost, considering how crowded the rest of the city is? Eli tries not to think about it.

Cixi cheeps, tugging again on her jesses. Kai rolls his eyes, then takes a roll of string out of his bag.

"There," he says, tying the string to one leg and letting her go, a streak of green-blue blurring into the sky. "I swear, if she manages to tangle herself up, I might just leave her there."

"You're not worried about her?" Eli asks, pointing at Qinglu.

"Qinglu's bribable," Kai says, scratching a hand over the dragon's shoulders. "She's also skittish about being in the city at all, so I'm more concerned about getting her to leave than to return. Not that it isn't understandable," he says, patting Qinglu's side. "Great big city, a lot to see for such a small dragon, isn't it?"

Qinglu hums, leaning into Kai's touch. Eli reaches one hand over, lets Qinglu sniff it briefly before scratching beneath her chin.

Such uninterrupted tranquility is an oddity, with night-clubs and bars undoubtedly full a few districts away. But surrounded by high-rises in the middle of an empty park within a gated community, it's easy to forget that. The rest of Beijing, at least temporarily, seems to fade away.

They walk the grounds for a while, neither saying any-thing. No one else enters the park, no harried manager comes out to scold them for trespassing. The buildings are tall and white and empty, the few lighted windows noticeable and small against the dark. It is almost eerie, this stillness, but somehow, walking with Kai, Eli isn't bothered.

Above them, Cixi is a child's drawing of a dragon as she flits in and out of low cloud cover. Kai frowns, seeing her, and tugs on the string; Cixi glances down, and blithely continues ignoring him. Kai rolls his eyes, then tugs again, and this time Cixi pulls back, veering hard off in one direction as if to prove she can. "An actual demon," Kai sighs, but loosens his grip on the string, letting it extend to its full length.

"You aren't worried about the string breaking?"

"I've done this before," Kai says. "None of the other drag-ons have escaped. Besides," he says, shrugging as he steps up onto the curb, balancing on the edge, "if she's really that set on escaping, she can go. Pain in the ass, honestly. Practically not even worth keeping, even if some rich asshole eventually ends up buying her."

As if hearing them, Cixi veers sharply to one side, jerking the line nearly out of Kai's hands.

It's only a moment — one flicker of a second as Kai stumbles forward, barely a few inches before he catches himself. But before he can help himself, Eli steps toward him, one hand extended forward in aid.

"Are you —"

"I'm fine," Kai says, straightening to look levelly at him. "You can stop looking at me like I'm about to start convulsing."

"Have I been making you feel that way?"

"Occasionally, yes. Not all that time," Kai says, jumping back onto the sidewalk. "Which is a mercy. But more often than I'd like. I wasn't exaggerating. I'm not here for your pity."

"I didn't —"

"You didn't mean to make me uncomfortable. I know." Kai turns. Outlined by the streetlights behind them, his eyes gleam as they meet Eli's. "But you still feel sorry for me."

"I don't feel sorry for you," Eli says. "I want to help you."

"Same thing, isn't it?"

Cixi circles down, chittering her displeasure as she lands on Kai's shoulder. She bumps her head against his cheek, gesture less affectionate than imperious.

"Brat," Kai says, but he gives in, one hand reaching under her chin to scratch her. Cixi leans into Kai's touch, luxuriating in the attention, and then pointedly nips at the creance line tethering her to him. Kai rolls his eyes but complies, and once Cixi is unclipped she's shooting off into the air like a cerulean bullet. On Kai's glove, Qinglu watches with wide, fascinated eyes.

"Come on, then," Kai says, nudging Qinglu off his hand. She leaves his glove, uncertain at first as she hovers in the air above them. She turns, though, when Cixi nips at her, tendrils flattening against her head before bolting after the larger dragon. Kai smiles at the dragons chasing each other, a small, brief expression, before sitting down on one of the swings. Eli takes the swing next to him, fingers wrapping around the chains automatically. The ground is a plasticky rubber beneath them, thick black material to blunt the blow of falling, and he can't help but push his feet in, testing the give.

"When did you find out?" Eli asks.

"In the last third of spring semester. Ended up changing my summer plans a bit." Kai shrugs, swings a little back and forth. "Probably for the better, actually — don't know how long I could have continued before killing one of the stupid first-years I had to work with."

Mentally, Eli does the math. Even taking in the issue of belated diagnosis, that would place the disease progression at only a few months, maybe a year at most. Late stage one or early stage two most likely. Damage present but the spread still slow, steady but not yet terminal. Treatable even, given access to proper medical care.

Out loud, Eli asks, "and what did you tell your family?"

"What would *you* tell your family?"

"So they don't know."

"No," Kai says after a pause, voice quiet. "They don't."

"Are you going to tell them?"

"I meant to," Kai says, "when it first happened. I was going to, but then ..." Kai looks away, lips thin. "I don't want to talk about this."

Eli wants to protest, but there's a hard set to Kai's jaw that tells him not to push. Instead, they watch Cixi and Qinglu weave through the light poles. Cixi's long, fan-like wings give her a clear speed advantage, but she slows her pace whenever Qinglu falls behind.

"Your parents," Kai asks, eyes still on the dragons above their heads. "How did they meet?"

"PhD program." Eli glances over, frowning. "Why do you ask?"

"Curiosity," Kai says, shrugging. "If it's going to be a night of personal questions, I think I should have a turn too."

"My life's not that interesting, I should warn you."

"Probably not," Kai agrees. "Most people's lives aren't once you know them. I don't know you, though."

"Okay," Eli says. Above them, Qinglu and Cixi are twin pinpoints, bright darts of color weaving figure eights against the dark sky. "My parents met at grad school, at some mixer. Mom was studying law and Dad was doing something with computers or engineering, and they hit it off. The typical grad student love story. They got married and had me before realizing they were better off being friends. Dad lives in London now, teaches computer science. He tries to visit, but he's busy and the tickets aren't cheap. So my mom and grandma raised me. It used to bother me when I was younger, but I don't mind it now."

"Fathers are like that," Kai says, and there's something in the way he says it that has Eli glancing at him, but Kai's gaze has already turned back to the ground. Eli wonders what would have happened if he had turned in time, what expression he would have found on Kai's face.

Instead, he asks, "how do you know so much about dragons?"

"Why do you want to know?"

"You asked a question," Eli points out. "It's my turn now."

"I studied biology," Kai says. "Of course I'd know about basic veterinary care."

"Yes, but ..." Eli shakes his head. "There are biology students in our lab, some of them on their master's or PhD, but they still don't — their knowledge is mostly theoretical, I guess, while yours ... it feels more familiar. Like you've spent time patching up dragons before, not just studied it in books."

"Or maybe the students you've met are just astonishingly incompetent? You're not wrong, though." Kai frowns, pushes slowly back and forth on his swing, metal creaking with every movement. "My parents lived in the countryside — well, it was a small town, really, but close enough to bicycle to the country. We were close to a wildlife rehabilitation center, run by a local Buddhist temple. I used to spend a lot of time there as a kid, watching the nuns take care of the dragons. I was eight, maybe nine when they started letting me help."

"That's very young. You didn't have, I don't know, friends you would rather play with?"

"Not many." Kai adjusts his position on the swing, eyes tracking Cixi as she swoops through the air. Not far behind, Qinglu blows a gust of air at her, knocking Cixi off course before she rights herself with a squawk of indignation. "I was a strange child."

I can imagine, Eli thinks but does not say. "I spent most of my childhood in the library."

That earns a snort of amusement. "College professor parents will do that, I imagine."

"College professor parents," Eli agrees solemnly. "Don't try it, you'll only end up with impossibly high academic standards and books for friends."

"I'll keep that in mind," Kai says. Above them, Cixi and Qinglu have settled into a game of diving at each other, twisting away from impact at the last second. It's a gentler version of the behavior Eli's seen in dragon fights, play with no real intent beyond the joy of stretching wings through air.

"Why are you here?" Kai asks.

"What?" Eli asks. "Do you mean existentially?"

"If you want to answer that, sure," Kai says. "But you know what I mean."

He does, of course. "Why do you want to know?"

"Curiosity," Kai says, shrugging. "And you're not ... all the other students in your program, they're here because they think it's somehow good for them or they want an extended vacation. But you, you're different ..."

"I don't look Chinese, I know."

"No. But you're not Chinese, are you? You're American."

"Afro-Chinese-American. It's a mouthful."

"Exactly," Kai says. "China is — it's a strange country, when it comes to differences. America and Europe — they're not perfect, I know, and I'm sure it hasn't been easy, being the type of person you are in America, but at least you still have more kinds of people there. In China, it's mostly just us.

Chinese people — Han people if you want to be precise. But even that's not completely accurate, not when you take Uighurs and other ethnic minorities into account the way most people don't. But the point is, even in cities like Shanghai and Hong Kong, there aren't that many foreigners, and when there are, you notice them. It's easy to tell when someone is different, and we're not good with differences here."

"Neither is America. I don't think it's a national thing."

Kai laughs at that, short and surprised. "Probably not," he says, and when he turns to Eli, he's smiling — wry, a little sharp around the edges, but genuine. "Unfortunately."

Kai swings a little. "You never answered the question. Why you're here."

"Didn't I?" Eli asks, pushing back with his feet. "I told you, I had the time and I wanted to do something useful with it."

"And you could have done all that in America, at any of the universities there. In a country that, okay, isn't perfect but is at least familiar. Why Beijing?"

It's the same question his mother and friends had asked, when they had heard, and the rehearsed answers are still there, words ready on the tip of his tongue. *The opportunity to work with world-class faculty — the hope of contributing useful research on a leading problem in medicine —*

"I'm not sure I know either, honestly," Eli says. "My family — my mother's side, at least — has a lot of history in this city, but we've never visited. It's always been Guilin or Shenzhen, one of the other cities where my relatives live now. So I guess coming here, being in the city where my mom and grandma grew up ... it felt right, I guess. I don't know."

"Do you still feel that? About being here, I mean."

Eli lifts his feet off the ground, lets his momentum carry him a few inches forward. "Sometimes, yes. I guess I'm still figuring it out."

Qinglu has landed on top of their swing set, and is occupied with licking the dust off her forelegs, but Cixi continues gliding above them, wings winking green and bright in the dim glow of city light. So high above, she becomes an almost abstract thing, a movement of constellation shapes against the sky.

It's impossible, but despite the light pollution and smog, Eli thinks he can almost make out some stars.

"Come on," Kai says after a few minutes, dusting himself off as he stands up. He whistles and pulls a few strips of jerky out of a pocket. Qinglu flies down immediately and Cixi, lured by the food and the loss of her playmate, follows a minute later. "We should get back."

"Your friend's been looking for you," Mr. Lin says.

"My friend?" Kai asks, not glancing up from his sketchbook.

"Your friend. You know, that American boy? He's been stopping by in the evenings. Not saying anything, just hanging around looking tall and hopeful." Mr. Lin lights a cigarette, cupping the flame between his hands. "Might want to see what he wants."

"He has my phone number. He'd let me know if it was anything serious." Still, it doesn't surprise Kai that Eli's been staking out the shop. For all his attempts at subtlety, Eli is about as stealthy as the packages of tea and lozenges that keep finding their way into the bags of dragon food and veterinary supplies they'd agreed upon as payment. It's deeply exasperating, as many things about Eli are, yet Kai can't help but also find it oddly endearing.

Mr. Lin gives him a look, the type that, when they first met, spoke volumes about what he thought of him, some nineteen-year-old college student offering to treat the wheezing cough of several of Mr. Lin's helong. It's a look Mr. Lin

54

directs mostly at the other employees these days, but it never quite lost its power to make Kai feel all of twelve years old.

"What?" Kai asks.

"Not really polite, leaving him to wait after you like that."

"If it's an emergency, he can send me a message. I'll ask him the next time we meet."

Mr. Lin makes a non-committal noise. Cigarette smoke wafts between them, slowly dissipating into the evening air. Mr. Lin's eyes are sharp as he watches Kai, making Kai instinctively bristle, but Mr. Lin keeps his thoughts to himself.

When he gets home, Kai thinks, turning his pencil to the side to shade in lamplit shadows, he should text Eli his hours. Stop him from hanging around the shop every other evening at least.

Lab ends early on Monday, the result of several botched petri solutions and a temporarily broken flow cytometer. Not quite wanting to accompany his lab mates to the bar and with nothing else to do, Eli makes his way to Mr. Lin's shop.

Kai isn't there.

Eli stands in front of the shop, staring at the lines of tanks and wooden stools, then goes inside.

"Excuse me," he says as he approaches Mr. Lin, who is sitting at the counter drinking tea as he scowls at a newspaper. "Do you know where Kai is?"

"Kai?" Mr. Lin looks up from his newspaper. "Kid doesn't work today."

Eli blinks.

"But he said —"

"Kid probably says all sorts of shit." Mr. Lin shrugs, taking a measured sip of his tea. "Doesn't mean he's getting paid for it. Kai wants to come in on Monday and stop my other employees from fucking up, I'm not going to stop him."

"Oh." Eli pauses to process this information. "So is he sick, or — do you know why —"

"No idea," Mr. Lin says, shrugging. "Usually shows, but I can't exactly go off on him for not being here when he isn't supposed to be, can I? Not my job to babysit him. Kid works for me, not the other way around."

Which is logical. Logical, of course, that Kai would be busy, would have other things to tend to and would, once in a while, miss a day or two of work —

In his textbooks, Eli remembers seeing pictures of shaolong's effects on the body, autopsies with black lungs cut open to show the extent of the damage, the delicate calligraphies of dark smoke twining through veins and capillaries. He remembers staring at the photo and rereading descriptions of end-stage patients, mentally comparing his memories of his grandmother against established diagnostic standards. His grandmother had never seemed in terrible pain during her last months, but she had also always hated making other people worry. Had she covered up inflamed skin and purpling bruises with makeup and long sleeves, scheduled her video calls to coincide with her days of health? Or had Eli simply not seen, too preoccupied with his work and his desire to see his grandmother well that he'd missed the signs of her health worsening? And has he made that mistake again here, in Beijing with Kai?

Eli swallows, forcing his voice steady. "Do you know where he lives, then?"

Mr. Lin raises an eyebrow. "You know," he says, "those type of questions get people suspicious. All I know, you could be part of some gang, here to cut him up or sell him for money." He sips his tea, then sighs when he sees Eli's face. "Joke, kid, wasn't going to call the cops on you, my god — three streets down, take a left, then the ugly block on Tong Alley. 1841C. Make sure he hasn't died on us, yeah?"

Kai gives himself ten seconds, counting backwards, then opens his eyes. But nothing has changed in the sparse apartment in front of him. The dragons still need him.

So Kai lowers his goggles, checks his gloves, and begins again.

His kitchen table has been repurposed into a makeshift examination counter for the occasion, brown butcher paper serving as both exam table paper and a tarp on the floor below. On an adjacent chair, Kai lays out the bandages in neat rows, then the cotton swabs next to them. On his shoulder, Mei wrinkles her nose, pulling back at the sight of the familiar tools.

"It's all right," Kai says, stroking her head. "They're not for you."

The first dragon hisses when he reaches into the tank, talons curling onto the edge of the glass lid when he gently lifts the creature up. Suspended in midair, the helong struggles in his grasp, its long body a grey-blue rope swinging in pendulum arcs. It makes him smile a little; a few hours in freshwater, and the river dragon is already spirited enough to be territorial. A fighter, this one. Kai hopes it will survive.

He is less certain about the others.

Three years of pouring over diagrams for zoology exams and dissecting animals for anatomy labs — the culmination of an interest sparked by a childhood spent watching volunteers sew up wounded wildlife at the Ren Ai Temple. All that so his hands would not shake when he handles the needle, pulling thread through scaly skin. He still fumbles a few times, the needle jerking as the dragons struggle against the anklets and leashes holding them in place. One of the larger hailong twists before he can get the leash over its head, snapping at his face with teeth as sharp as needles. But Kai moves quickly enough that the wound is only a scratch, and afterwards, Mei clicks so angrily that the larger dragon is shamed into stillness.

She's still hissing when he puts away his supplies, a low, steady sibilance that persists even when the hailong has rolled into a ball inside the tank. "It's all right, Mei," he whispers, tickling under her chin, "I'm fine, see?"

Mei curls her tail around Kai's bicep but keeps a baleful eye on the hailong, clearly skeptical of Kai's ability to protect himself. Kai remembers a time when she could curl her entire body around his wrist like a bracelet, a grey dragonet he'd snuck into the dorms, swearing his roommates to secrecy. Barely larger than a city sparrow and with scales not yet hardened to adult toughness, she'd been fearless even then, darting at mice and birds twice her size whenever Kai took her out for flight practice. Little wonder that she's so headstrong as an adult.

Gently stroking Mei's head, Kai glances down. There's blood on the floor, most of it on the butcher paper but some finding its way onto the tiles. He'll have to scrub it later, before the stains can set.

Kai closes his eyes, allows himself that one small, brief luxury. Then he stands up and, brushing the dust off his clothes, goes outside.

It's bright out. Hot. Heat speeds evaporation, makes wet, scaly skin dry out faster than flowers in the sun. Kai, plastic bag full of bloodied rags in one hand, doesn't like to think what would have happened if he had woken up later, if he had taken the other route to work instead of passing by the trash collection bins.

He sees no more bags or boxes or anything that could contain a dragon as he approaches the row of dumpsters and recycling bins now, at least. That is a small mercy. Dragon meat and leather may be illegal and still near-sacrilege to consume or procure, but Kai doubts that Beijing's street dogs and scavengers care much for ancient theology.

"Kai!"

He starts, turns, and of course it's him.

"Kai!" Eli calls again, slowing to a stop. He's breathing hard, thin T-shirt almost translucent with sweat and eyes feverishly bright. "What are you doing here?"

"Taking the trash out," Kai says. "I took the day off. What are *you* doing here?"

"I thought — our lab finished early this morning, so I thought I would visit. But then you weren't at the store, and I was worried that —"

He trails off then, gaze darting over Kai as if unsure he is still there. Not for the first time, Kai resents that Eli's height means he needs to look up to meet his eyes. Involuntarily, Kai feels his hands clench, and he thrusts them into his pockets before Eli can see.

"Thank you for your concern, but as you can see," he says, "I haven't dropped dead yet. You can go now. I'm sure you're busy."

Eli blinks. "I wasn't trying to — I just wanted — I'm sorry —"

By all rights, Kai should be angry. And on some level, he supposes he *is* angry. He's angry that Eli has followed him all this way, angry that Eli has found him here after that one inadvertent stumble from the store to this apartment, this godforsaken mess he had scrabbled to afford so that no one, not even his friends, would ever find him.

But when he looks at Eli, the disheveled hair, the brown eyes blinking in confusion, Kai feels no anger, only deep weariness.

"Or," he says, sighing, "you could come inside and have some tea."

"Stay here," Kai says. He places a hand against Eli's chest as they stand outside his door. "I'll get you shoes."

He closes the door, leaving Eli alone in the dim hallway.

"Okay, you can come in," Kai says when he opens the door, handing Eli a pair of blue-and-yellow sandals. "It's a little cleaner now."

"You didn't have to do anything," Eli says. Kai holds the sandals out between them. "It's fine, I wasn't planning to stay —"

Kai stares at him.

Flushing, Eli takes the shoes.

Kai's apartment is small, bare. Sweat beads on the back of Eli's neck, the dry heat of the outdoors fading into the muggier warmth inside. A bed by one wall, a kettle in the corner, next to a small heap of sketches. Layered one on top of another, the colors and forms blur so that Eli can only catch pieces of images: a glimpse of a foreleg, the edge of a claw reaching toward some star or stretch of sky. Toward the middle of the room, there's a table covered by a long sheet of paper — an art project, maybe? Or perhaps Kai hadn't seen the point in spending money on a tablecloth. No art on the walls, no carpet to cover cracked floor tiles — not a sign of excess except for the tanks and cages spread throughout the room and the small, jewel-bright dragons inside.

Kai emerges from the kitchen, a cup of tea in one hand. "Here," Kai says. "Drink. You've had pu-erh?"

"It's all right," Eli says, shaking his head, "you don't have to — I'll just —"

"Please," Kai says. "I insist."

They sip their tea, Kai's eyes never quite leaving Eli.

"They're all very beautiful," Eli says to break the silence, nodding at the dragons around them. "Are they all yours?"

Kai sips his tea as he considers the question. "You could say that," he says. "In a way."

"In a way?"

"They're not pets, if that's what you mean," Kai says. "God no, you think I'd actively want a dozen of these terrors around … it's a temporary thing. They were there and they needed help, so I took them in. Someone needed to."

Eli's confusion must show, because Kai sighs, crossing his arms as he holds Eli's gaze. Eli notices, suddenly, how dark the bags under Kai's eyes are, how tired he looks.

"Dragons," Kai says, voice level, "aren't cheap — not the ones people like to keep as pets, at least. City dragons, they've been around Beijing for centuries so they've had time to adapt, like foxes or sparrows. Imports, though, are delicate creatures, finicky as hell about salinity levels and so high-strung it makes you wonder why rich people like them so much. I think it's something to do with some drama about a pop star who also had superpowers. It was out several years ago — anyway, it doesn't matter. The main character had a talking dragon for a pet, and since the actress was popular then, it became a fad — everyone wanted a dragon too. But then, with the drought people started realizing what they'd bought. The more conscientious ones," he says, shrugging, "they'll take them to a river or a lake, somewhere out of town. The rest — the animal shelters are overfull as it is, and it's not like there are many people who'd want an aquatic pet right now. So I do. When I can."

"Oh," Eli says, fumbling for words. "That's a very generous thing to do."

Kai smiles thinly. Leans forward, picks up the teapot and refills his cup before glancing up at Eli with a look that was polite. Neutral.

"More tea?"

"All right," Eli says. Now that he looks closer, he can see the wads of cotton, the difficulty with which some of these dragons move through their tanks. There are scars — thick, old lines crisscrossing delicate wing tissue and armored scales. Some of the scars — some of the worst ones — are newer, red and shiny around the edges. And then those lines of stitches, the red bleeding through some of those bandages ...

When Eli was eleven or twelve and walking home from soccer practice, he'd stumbled on a box of kittens, each so small he could hold them in one hand. His mother's allergies meant that they couldn't keep them, and as they drove to the nearest no-kill shelter, Eli remembers staring at the box and its tiny contents. The kittens must have been barely a week old; only a few of them had opened their eyes, and even as his grandmother directed him on how to gently rub their stomachs to keep the kittens warm, Eli had been half-certain they would die before they reached the shelter. Even after the vet tech on duty had proclaimed the kittens underweight but otherwise well and thanked Eli's mother for coming in so quickly, he hadn't been able to stop thinking about it — about how small the kittens were, and how he'd only found them because he'd gone to recycle his water bottle and heard meowing from inside the dumpster. Someone must have put those kittens into that box and that dumpster, seen these small helpless things and decided that it was simply too much time and effort to, what? Let their pet cat raise her own kittens? Put up 'for sale' ads or simply drive to the nearest animal shelter?

He hadn't understood it then. Standing in Kai's apartment, staring at Kai's dragons and the record of deliberate cruelty written across their skin, he doesn't understand it now.

Kai finishes pouring and places a steaming cup of tea in front of him. Kai's hands, when they reach for his own tea, are dry and faintly red, the scrubbed rawness that comes from too much work and not enough care. Sitting with his hands wrapped around a chipped teacup, Kai is all sharp lines and shadows, dark circles under his eyes and healing scratches on one arm. Like looking at a charcoal sketch, there but ready to smudge into blackness at an uncareful touch.

"Is there —" Eli says, then stops, starts again. "Is there anything I can do?"

Kai glances up then, eyes catching Eli's. "I'm sorry?"

"I just ..." Eli shrugs, not sure how to begin. "Everything you've been describing, the abuse, the cruelty — and it's just you. You're doing it all alone and ... it's not right. If there's any way I can, I want to help. If there's anything you need, if there's anything I can do or I can get you —"

"I've already been taking the supplies I need from your lab. It's kind of you to offer, but it's all right. I'm fine."

"But it's not fair. You shouldn't be the only one —"

"Fair?" Kai asks, raising one eyebrow. "Of course it's not fair. We're in one of the richest cities in the world, and there are people starving in the streets, businessmen spending thousands of yuan to cheat on their wives and feeling generous for giving a few coins to a beggar. You think anyone cares about *fair*?"

"You do," Eli points out. "I do."

"Oh, good," Kai says, "two people in a city of millions. Truly encouraging, I look forward to seeing how we single-handedly turn years of corruption and systemic injustice around."

"I'm not talking about that, though," Eli says, leaning forward. "I'm talking about here and now, this one problem and what we can do to make it better. And it wouldn't be impossible — it wouldn't even be that hard. Dr. Wang is always talking about how much she wants to carry out more experiments but how the department is hesitant about the cost. But if we offered them this, a pool of subjects readily available for free —"

He stops, aware of the odd way Kai is eyeing him.

"Thank you," Kai says. "Again, that's kind of you to offer. But please, you needn't bother."

"But it wouldn't be a bother," Eli says. "All I would have to do is ask Dr. Wang and I can't see her saying no, not when it would help Beida too. It'd be so easy —"

"Perhaps," Kai says, shrugging. "But I'd rather do without any more of your charity."

"Charity? This isn't about charity, or pity, or — look," he sighs, running a hand over his hair in frustration as he stands up. "I'm just trying to help you —"

"Are you?" Kai asks, eyes flashing as he stands up to match Eli. "Are you sure about that, *really* sure, that you're doing this out of pure good will? That you don't have some other motive, some other reason you're here?"

"I don't —"

"Are you sure?"

Silence, falling like rain on concrete.

They're so close now, close enough that Eli can see the bloody dots from torn capillaries on Kai's cheeks, the outline of each individual eyelash as it curls against pale skin. And suddenly Eli realizes the reason he had been so riveted the night of those fights, the reason he had come back to the store afterwards, the reason he had found himself lingering after each meeting, hoping for a word or glance more —

They hold the gaze too long, and then Kai flushes, turns away.

"Kai —"

"Don't," Kai says, shaking Eli's hand off his shoulder. "I think you should leave."

Eli stares at him.

"Kai," he begins. "I —"

But nothing comes out. All language deserts him. No English, no Chinese — nothing now but a stop in his throat, a heaviness on his tongue.

Kai's mouth is set and his eyes are averted. But Eli waits, watching his dark eyes, the long lashes, the thin, delicate line of Kai's neck. Watches, as if observing a science experiment, as red fans across his face, the flush blooming like the unfurling petals of a peony.

Eli leans over. Slowly, carefully, telegraphing every movement so as not to startle, to give Kai time to change his mind and turn away, he brings his mouth down.

After the Dragons

Kai's lips are dry when they meet his, chapped and harsh. Tasting of dried blood and unnaturally, feverishly hot.

4

Monday is a Public Wellness day.

Mr. Lin texts him Sunday night: *if I see you tomorrow, I'm firing you.* It's an unnecessary warning; like everyone else, Kai gets the alerts on his phone, and even if he hadn't, the announcements blared from speakers in every public square. *Dear citizens, tomorrow's weather reports indicate high levels of air pollution. Sensitive groups should stay indoors, and all citizens are encouraged to reduce outdoor activity. Masks and other supplies will be available at all government health centers. For more information on how to locate your nearest health center, please visit our official website at w w w dot —*

A few months ago, Kai would have heard the alert, fished around his drawers for a face mask, and gone about his day, maybe stopped by Mr. Lin's shop just to test the seriousness of his threat. Now, Kai closes the windows, sets up his government-issued air purifier and humidifier, and checks the Ministry of Ecology and Environment's official Beijing app. One of the Ecological and Environmental Protection Mascots, a big-eyed cartoon character with a leaf in its hair and an oversized head topped with hill-like peaks, smiles cheerfully back at him, unrepentant in its abject cuteness. *Purple Alert from 6:00-17:59, Red Alert predicted from 18:00-23:59. Working together, we stay safer!* No chance of an evening reprieve, then — red might be more tolerable than purple, but Kai has learned from experience that it's best not to test his luck on days like this.

Kai refills food and water bowls, cleans cages, checks tank settings, and mentally organizes today's adjustments: change the water for this tank, add more aquarium salt for this one, clean the filter for that one. Water is included in Kai's rent, but between getting charged for anything above the municipal individual usage limit and the "Warning: Monthly Drought Quota Exceeded" notices his landlord has been passive-aggressively leaving on his door, Kai has learned to be creative about water usage. Librarians eye him and his oversized backpack suspiciously, but so long as Kai sticks to refilling water bottles in the bathroom and not stealing books, he can avoid their wrath. Besides, libraries are public facilities — Kai isn't doing anything illegal, and certainly nothing worse than the downtown luxury hotels that blatantly flout drought regulations with their glittering fountains and lush watered lawns.

There are no major injuries in his current group of rescues, so it's a cursory round of making sure none of the dragons have pulled their stitches or tried to chew off their bandages. Kai supposes he could do laundry or tackle the water stains in his bathroom, but he's already spent most of his morning running errands and he only has so much patience for housework. With all the immediate tasks done and the day stretching out before him, Kai drags out his canvas and easel, and settles into an afternoon of Public Wellness.

He has a rhythm when he paints, a steady, three-step movement the brush follows as it moves across the canvas — one, two, three, stop. Stand back, look down, appraise the colors on the canvas. If necessary, dab the excess, add another touch of green or yellow. Then stand back again, brush at the ready, and one, two, three. One, two, three.

It's a learned routine, more than anything. When he was young, painting was a different kind of activity: all furious, messy strokes and a rush to get colors on canvas as they appeared in his head. "Careful," his father had laughed, whenever he had caught him at it, sleeves rolled and paint flecked over his face. "Don't want to ruin another shirt, do you? Don't think your mother will appreciate that."

Now, however, Kai's strokes are quick but deliberate, every move a small, ordered part of a larger whole. One, two, three. Father, mother, sister.

Occasionally, he glances down at his sketches, wrinkled and leaning against the windowsill. Eli's face looks back at him, eyes solemn and sincere from a panoply of paper.

It's stupid. He knows it is, had known it even as he found himself drawing the pictures — a thousand blurred drawings hidden in the back of notebooks and sketch pads, hastily shoved away whenever anyone approached. He'd been in relationships before, even had a few almost serious partners between one-night stands and more casual flings, and yet he'd never been sentimental about them. Eli had kissed him, yes, but so have a half dozen straight boys—some under the influence of alcohol, others driven by simple curiosity. Eli is a foreign exchange student, by definition here only for a few months; the whole thing is ephemeral, with no chance of lasting longer than a summer —

And yet Eli's lips had been soft when they kissed, hands large but gentle as they moved up and down his back. His body was a warm weight against Kai's as they lay facing each other on Kai's twin mattress, talking late into the night. Kai wakes up warm most days, an inevitable side effect of a hot summer without air conditioning combined with his chronic illness, but it's been a long time since he's woken up with someone next to him. Asleep, Eli had looked so young, face free for once from the stubborn concern he wears in the stiff set of his mouth and the faint, ever-present furrow between his brows. In the pale-yellow light of morning, the day unfurling around them, it had been easy for Kai to push away his earlier irritation and read Eli's concern as touching instead of condescending. Kai can take care of himself, has been doing so since he was a child, but there's a small, childish part of him comforted by the possibility of not having to. It's a pretty daydream, something to fold away and keep for rainy days. Kai isn't naïve enough to mistake it for life.

Kai swallows, then forces his focus back to the painting in front of him. One, two, three. Mother, father, sister. If he thinks of it in terms of technique, composition and necessary steps, he can push it away, the premature nostalgia driving him to do this, create some souvenir of what he knows is necessarily temporary.

One, two, three. And then step back, gauge the play of color and lines.

Warm tan skin and softly curling hair, high cheekbones on a long, sharp face. All the pieces that make up 'Elijah Ahmed' present, but something still missing, some ineluctable quality not yet captured in the strokes of oil on canvas.

"It's the eyes," his father says from behind him. Kai is struck, as always, by how young his father is in these visions, face as yet unlined by the years of factory work that would eventually seep a cocktail of toxins into his veins. The company had paid the funeral costs, a kind of sheepish apology for causing his father's death in the first place, but the damage had been too much for the morticians to fully fix. "The way he watches the world, quiet and careful, or the way he looks at you. You're almost there, yes, but could you really leave it like that? Stop work on something when it's so close to finished?"

"Stop it," Kai says, dipping his brush into a pool of white paint. "I know."

No response.

And that, Kai thinks as he sits back, surveying the canvas in front of him, is just like his father — loving, encouraging, and yet enigmatic to the last. In death as in life.

One, two, three. Mother, sister, mother.

Kai stands back, squints at the canvas in the bright sun.

Almost. But not quite.

69

It's late morning when the train arrives, screeching to a stop in a spray of dust. This far out from the city center, the sky is startlingly blue, the sun cutting a bright swathe through the summer air.

The lone attendant leaning against a telephone pole looks up when he reaches the gates, meeting Eli's nod with one of his own before returning to his phone.

The grass crunches beneath his feet as Eli traces the worn path to his destination, a familiar sequence of left, right, then two more steps right, and then *there*, by the old gingko tree with the peeling bark. Without speaking, he stands over the familiar stone and plot of grass, hands in his pockets.

"Hi, grandma," he says finally.

His grandmother's tombstone faces him, silent as ever.

There are peonies on the grave, red and still fresh; an old student or admirer he thinks as he picks them up, turning the flowers in his fingers. Even in Massachusetts, with her auto-didact English thickened by a Beijing accent, his grandmother had had a way with people. She'd debated with his mother's students and Oxbridge-educated colleagues with a confidence unhindered by her lack of anything more than a high school diploma and a handful of college credits. Years teaching high schoolers will make you good at projecting authority, Eli supposes. But even so, he'd always admired that about her, the easy assurance she and his mother exuded but which had somehow skipped over him. By all accounts, Eli had been an awkward, shy child, preferring to play by himself instead of with the other kids at daycare, and that tendency toward solitude had only increased with age. As in all things, his mother has been his staunchest ally, defending Eli against playground bullies and casually bigoted remarks from relatives with a ferocity that had been frankly a little mortifying. But there are times when Eli catches his mother studying him like a court ruling she is trying to unravel. His mother loves him; this Eli has never doubted. But he can't help but wonder if she had anticipated everything that came with him. Letting go of his

70

father had been a strategic choice, a mutual decision to salvage what was left of a once-warm friendship instead of becoming one of those bitter couples whose children silently wish for divorce. But Eli knows his mother had a steep learning curve in the beginning. She had been prepared to take on the world for him, but even she could not have anticipated all the ways it would come for them, a working single mother and a son whose dark skin provoked comments from strangers who assumed they couldn't be related. She had done her best, tackling critical race theory with the fervor of an overachieving grad student. But in the end, there were some things theory could not prepare her for.

A few leaves have fallen on his grandmother's grave. Eli brushes them off with a hand and then stays there, squatting on his haunches in front of her stone.

"Sorry I haven't visited." It feels a little strange, talking out loud, like acting a scene out from a movie, but no one is there to see him. He isn't religious — none of his family has ever been — but he thinks there might be something to it, a chance that his presence here, his words out loud, might reach her. "Things have been ... busy."

He can't help but smile at how utterly inadequate that description is. Memories of the last week bubble up: scratchy sheets and cold tea, sharing space on furniture clearly meant for one and the unexpected pleasure of waking up against a familiar body in an unfamiliar bed. Kai smiling to himself in the morning light, and trying to hide it when he sees Eli watching; Kai's hands as he pours tea, chapped and calloused and mapped by small scars but elegant for all that, fingers long and strong; Kai sketching under low light, frowning as he erases a line, sighing but capitulating as he tilts the paper for Eli to see, then tilts his mouth up for a kiss.

Distinctly aware that he is remembering these things while in front of his grandmother's grave, Eli forces his thoughts away.

"I have some stuff for you," he says, untying the plastic bag he brought with him. He takes the offerings out one by one, so that she can see. His grandmother had taught him this, when he was young and had watched her light incense in front of his grandfather's shrine, explaining each item as she laid it out on the lacquer altar. Piles of doll-sized paper clothing and cardboard furniture, so that they would not want for anything in the afterlife; wine and sweets, so that they would not go hungry; incense, so that the dead could see that they were missed and hear the messages of those they had left behind.

He hasn't brought much joss paper with him. Despite her experiences with scarcity during the Great Chinese Famine, his grandmother had always been disdainful of a people who hoarded money as though banknotes were a talisman against misfortune. *Banknote's a piece of fancy paper,* she'd told him once, talking about those hard years of hunger. *You can buy rice with it, yes, but when there's no one selling you can't make soup out of hundred yuan notes.* Given the popularity of joss paper, Eli doubts the afterlife has caught up with his grandmother's peasant practicality — but perhaps it has, and billions of fake yuan are still floating in the ether somewhere, useless to the dead. Either way, Eli has elected to bring laopo bing and hard sesame candy, a few of the foods she had enjoyed while she was alive. A few paper iPhones, printed off a library computer and cut out along blocky lines, because she had always hated smartphones when she was alive and he thinks she would enjoy the thought of him burning them here. Fresh flowers because no matter where his grandmother was, she had never been able to live without color.

Finally, he lights the incense. The scents of jasmine and magnolia drift through the air as the smoke rises into the sky, a thin, shifting column of white. Attracted by either the food or the scent of incense, a small tianlong hovers above his grandmother's grave. Its moss-green body with brown stripes camouflages the creature against the background of trees. Eli tosses a piece of pastry in the air, and the dragon catches it, chirping appreciatively before flitting away. Sitting cross-legged in front of his grandmother's grave, Eli watches the incense smoke float heavenwards and wonders what messages are being sent to the dead. From wherever she is, does his grandmother hear his words, both the said and the unsaid? What would she think of him here, in her city with all his hazy hopes?

"I met someone, actually," he says, watching the sticks burn. "You and mom were always getting on my case about it, wondering when I'd finally meet a nice girl, and guess what? Turns out I wasn't even into girls in the first place."

He laughs at that a little. It's not funny, but he can't help it, thinking of how many years it's taken him to get here. While his friends had complained about curfews and the necessity of arranging clandestine meetings to see their girlfriends, his mother and grandmother had nudged him to talk with the nice Asian girls at community potlucks. *Too serious,* his mother had told him, *and that's good, sweetheart. We're glad we don't have to worry, but you need to learn to have a little fun.* And he had tried — half curiosity, half obligation to some sub-conscious ideal of what teenage boys were supposed to like — but every experiment had felt perfunctory, kissing an action that never quite lived up to the movie adaption. It'd been a long couple years of basement make-out sessions and burning morning-after embarrassment, but some time into his second year of college, Eli had finally let it go. He'd settled somewhere between tentative asexuality and *not the right person yet* — a bit of a puzzling grey area, yes, but ultimately nothing to lose sleep over. When his housemates came stumbling home from messy breakups and ill-advised hookups, Eli had been sympathetic, pouring out coffee and nodding along to whatever complaints were the issue du jour, but there had always been a sense of distance, the feeling of watching everything happen through a pane of glass. A gap between himself and them, romance and all its Shakespearean passion a territory he had resigned himself to never quite understand.

73

Now, though, this thing with Kai has changed everything. Technically, they've done little beyond kissing and sharing the same bed when Eli finds himself at Kai's at two in the morning. But it's so much more than he thought it would be, more than he thought he would ever want. This thing with Kai — whatever it is or whatever it turns out to be — feels like exploring a city without a map, the sweetness of unhurried wandering broken by bursts of vertiginous serendipity. Eli doesn't know if what he feels for Kai is the same feeling about which poets wrote so many odes, but he's curious now. He wants to find out, if there's time.

"He's ... different," he says to his grandmother's grave. "You'd like him, I think." He hopes she would, at the least. While he has few worries about his parents, growing up on college campuses where differences proliferated and were deliberately cultivated, he'd never discussed the issue with his grandmother — never had any reason to, the default assumption being that Eli was straight and merely a late bloomer. He likes to think, though, that his grandmother would have been kind about it. That, having been born during one revolution and lived through another, witness to a father torn apart for loyalty to old gods and a husband publicly spit on for Western decadence, she would have been kinder toward supposed deviance. That, even if she did not quite understand, she would have at least loved him through it. She would have liked Kai, he's certain. That fierce independence and stark sense of right and wrong — he can see his grandmother understanding that. Maybe even empathizing with it.

"I miss you," he says, because it is the type of thing you say here, the type of thing you can admit to the dead. "My current professor, she's working on shaolong, she's got theories on how studying draconic evolution might help us discover something new about the disease, some biological mechanism or wonder molecule that we can use to cure or prevent this. Dragons aren't supposed to do well in cities — and most don't. Toxins build up in tissue faster than most other animals. But the fact that some survive in the city makes Dr. Wang think draconic biology might be medically useful for human diseases tied to pollution. And I know it's a long shot and that even if Dr. Wang is right we'd still be nowhere close to a cure, but I wish ... I wish you could be here for it. I wish I could have helped."

On his grandmother's grave, the incense steadily burns, sweetening the air with the faint smell of flowers. It is a warm, sunny day, and though the grass is dry beneath him, it is still inviting. Eli could just lie down, close his eyes and let the day carry him along.

He stands up instead. Removes the sticks of incense from the holder, pouring water from his bottle over them to put the fire out before lining the sticks neatly on his grandmother's grave. A message, perhaps, if she can still receive it. *I'm sorry I couldn't be here earlier, with the rest of my family; I'm sorry I let myself get too busy to talk to you more when I had the chance. I hope you can forgive me.*

"I'll come back soon," he tells her, and it's a promise to himself as well.

It's a rare cool day when Eli leads Dr. Wang through the maze of streets to Kai's apartment. Kai is waiting outside as planned, lips pressed into a thin line as he watches their approach.

"Hi," he says, nodding at Eli. "Thank you for coming here," Kai directs this to Dr. Wang, who smiles in response. In her T-shirt and worn jeans, Dr. Wang could pass for a mother visiting her child. But her gaze is bright as she surveys the apartment building, mind almost audibly clicking along as she registers boarded-up windows and the broken stair railing lead up to Kai's place. "Come in."

They shuck their shoes off at the door. Kai's bought new house slippers, Eli notices, and feels briefly guilty for incurring this expense. Dr. Wang doesn't say anything about the bare walls or lack of air conditioning, and Eli is grateful for his professor's silence.

From her place atop a shelf, Mei chirps, stretching her head toward Dr. Wang in curiosity.

"Oh, hello," Dr. Wang says, glancing up. "Who are you, my pretty girl?"

"Her name is Mei," Kai says. "She's generally friendly, but I'd still watch my fingers. She gets protective sometimes."

"Hello, Mei," Dr. Wang says, lifting one hand for her investigation; after a few sniffs, Mei stretches her neck, an obvious bid for petting. "It's a pleasure to meet you, my dear." Mei warbles, and Dr. Wang gives her a conciliatory scratch before returning her attention to the rest of the room.

"I'm here," Dr. Wang says, nodding at Eli. "What now?"

Kai moves to the table and pulls out a chair. "We can start by sitting down."

As Eli and Dr. Wang take their seats around the kitchen table. Kai pours tea into new, unchipped cups. They sip cautiously as they wait for it to cool.

"All right," Eli says, when it seems like they have settled in. "I've talked to both of you about this already, but I think we should refresh some of it. So we're all on the same page. Dr. Wang, you've been wanting to explore draconic biology as a possible avenue for the development of new medical treatments, but the department is concerned about costs."

Eli gives a nod in Kai's direction. "Kai has worked extensively with dragons, both in the classroom and outside of it, and he's been informally helping Mr. Lin for a few years now. This summer, he's been taking in dragons and patching them up. Some of them go to Mr. Lin after they recover, but that leaves dozens more that aren't worth as much or are too hurt for most people to want to pay for. I've looked it up, and the cost of feeding dragons isn't much higher than keeping similar model organisms — most of the cost comes from the equipment and the initial expense of dragons themselves. Beida already has the equipment and Kai's willing to lend us dragons if we help with their medical upkeep. So if we worked together, it'd be mutually beneficial: less work for Kai, better care for the dragons, and a chance for Beida to do cutting-edge research at minimal cost."

Eli pauses, picks up his tea so that his hands have something to do as he glances from Kai to Dr. Wang. He hadn't memorized the speech per se, but he had gone over the points beforehand to make sure he had everything in order. He hopes, watching them now, that it would be enough.

"You know," Dr. Wang says, turning to Kai, "Eli can be incredibly stubborn, when he wants to be. You wouldn't guess it from looking at him, nice American boy that he is, but it's true. Cornered me after a lab one day and started talking about this idea of his. When I tried to explain how difficult getting departmental approval would be, he dug his heels in and wouldn't stop talking until I agreed to come."

"I know," Kai says, and for possibly the first time since they met, he smiles at Dr. Wang. "It's just as frustrating on this side."

"Hey," Eli says, but it's half-hearted. "It's worked out well, hasn't it? I've gotten you here."

"Yes," Dr. Wang says, meditatively sipping her tea. "You have. I haven't agreed to anything though."

"But you might. You wouldn't be here if you weren't thinking about it."

"True enough." Dr. Wang finishes the rest of the tea, puts her cup back on the table. "I can't make a decision without knowing what I'm agreeing to. Do you mind if I have a look at the dragons you currently have?"

Kai shrugs. "Go ahead."

A few cages line the walls, but Kai has moved the majority of them toward the bathroom, near the back door. Several of the cages have towels draped over them — "for the nocturnal and the shy ones," Kai had explained once, as the two of them watched over an injured panlong — and Dr. Wang is careful as she lifts the cloths. The dragons inside blink in the sudden brightness.

A few dragons stiffen at her approach, hiss when she hovers too close, but Dr. Wang is good at calming them, staying still and murmuring assurances.

Dr. Wang coaxes one of the friendlier tianlong onto her shoulder where the creature stretches his neck in an plea for affection. She scratches him with one hand, the other slowly unfolding one wing to examine it. There's a bandage on the dragon's chest, white and newly changed; Dr. Wang lifts it, revealing long gashes crisscrossing high between his two front legs, what Kai says is likely the result of a fight with a stray cat or another dragon. He's thin and the tips of his wings are tattered, but Eli remembers when Kai had first brought the tianlong in. The dragon had shivered with fear as Kai wiped the blood from his chest and legs, and Eli had hovered nearby until Kai snapped at him to either sit down or get him some proper bandages.

And now the small dragon Kai had refused to name (because *"it's harder, when you get attached"*) is nuzzling Dr. Wang's hand, letting her reposition him to better examine his scars.

"These aren't bad," Dr. Wang says, fingers tracing the stitches on an ugly gash across the tianlong's chest. "Did you do them yourself?"

Kai nods a dismissive *yes.* "Anatomy lessons, years of observation, and helping my mother with fixing old clothes. We had a few practicals in classes, but it's mostly experience."

"And you've been doing this for how long?"

"Off and on, over the years. Helped out with a local dragon rescue as a kid, where they eventually trained me, and then I started sneaking a few into my dorm my first year of college. We weren't allowed to have pets in the dorms, but well," Kai's gesture is unapologetic, "I always thought that was a stupid rule."

"I can see that," Dr. Wang murmurs, but her attention is on the tianlong in front of her. "How many new dragons would you say you get each week?"

"Depends. There's always abandoned dragons around, if you know where to look. Like Eli said, I give them to Lin when I can, the ones people would want for pets. But there are way more than he can sell. The others I've been taking out of the city and setting free in places approximating their natural environments — freshwater dragons by freshwater and salt-water dragons by the saltiest body of water available. It's maybe not the best choice environmentally since they're tech-nically still pets being introduced to a new habitat. But they're disturbing urban ecosystems if they stay in the city. At least in the country, they have a better chance than in Beijing."

"Understandable," Dr. Wang says. "Not an ideal solution, but the best one you can find." She stands up, smoothing her pants, and pulls out her phone. Wincing at the time, she turns back to Kai, Peking University Changjiang Distinguished Service Professor Dr. Wang Jiachun in full effect.

"The thing is," Dr. Wang says, "as irregular as it is, Eli does have a point — there would be some bureaucratic fuss, of course, but once we get past that, it would be quite a good situation for my team at Beida. And, well," she says, smiling as she slips the phone back in her pocket, "I've never been above taking advantage of a good opportunity."

Dr. Wang nods, and they sit back down to their tea. Negotiators gathered at a table, Eli thinks, glancing around.

"I can't take them in right away, of course — I can't imagine having to explain why we have an extra twenty drag-ons to the department head. But I've brought the issue up in meetings before, and I can't see my colleagues being too difficult once I explain the details to them. Like I said, there aren't that many studies on dragons right now, so this would be an exciting opportunity for us."

"All right," Kai says, once he's finished refilling their tea. "And then?"

"We're working out the particulars," Dr. Wang admits. "Immunology's not the only department interested in draconic research, and the more researchers we can get interested, the stronger our proposal will be. So far, we've got the wildlife researchers who want to study migration patterns and behaviors in the wild, the herpetologists and evolutionary biologists who are excited to build a database of the draconic genome, and the conservationists working with the Beijing Zoo who want ambassador animals to use with the general public. All this work will benefit us as well, even if maintaining equitable power and budget distributions will be a headache. That's a problem for another day. As it is, it'll be touch-and-go as we sort things out, but my prediction is that most dragons will pass through our lab briefly before being transferred to adoption or band-and-release programs in local wildlife centers."

Kai reaches back to pet Mei, wrapped like a snoozing, scaly scarf around his neck. "And what would you be doing with the dragons in the lab?"

Dr. Wang hums, tapping her fingers against her chin. "We'll begin with standard intake procedures — weight, wingspan, blood samples — and if other departments find something promising in that data, they'll take over research. We'll be sharing data across departments, but it does mean less responsibility for Immunology specifically. If no outstanding features present themselves during intake, we'll continue with rehabilitation, monitoring individual dragons in case any intriguing developments present themselves. Most of the day-to-day care will fall to the researchers in veterinary medicine, but my lab will be collaborating with them, both in terms of data analysis and developing experimental treatments for the dragons who have more extensive injuries or long-term conditions. It's a neat bit of symmetry — the eventual goal of this project is to apply draconic research to human diseases, but until we can do that, we'll be using insights from human medicine to treat dragons."

Dr. Wang pauses until Kai urges her on. The motion jostles Mei, and she opens her eyes to glare blearily at them before tucking her head beneath folded wings.

"Overall, while we would test some new medicines and treatment regimens on certain dragons to see if they speed recovery, what we're after is longitudinal, life-long data. That entails more waiting and watching than anything else. I know animal welfare is a concern of yours," Dr. Wang says with a nod at the cages of dragons, some missing eyes or limbs. "I can offer you my word that we'll treat our subjects well. Know that my goal with this project is to produce work that's useful for both veterinary and human medicine. Our researchers will be treating dragons as patients, and a doctor's first responsibility is always to their patient. This a lot to take on faith, but our goal here is to work with you, and that means making sure you're satisfied. You've already been working with our dragons, with Eli, and you can continue doing that in an official capacity. Quaint as your arrangement has been, Beida has money to pay one more student employee, and I'd rather not violate any labor laws while helping head this project."

"So I bring you dragons, you run tests while rehabilitating them, and I come in periodically to make sure you aren't cutting my dragons open," Kai summarizes. Shifting to a more comfortable position across Kai's shoulders, Mei lifts her head, yawns, and then resumes napping. "What happens if I get busy or have to leave Beijing or I'm," Kai pauses, thinking over his words before he continues, "otherwise unavailable?"

"I hope that you'd give us fair warning beforehand," Dr. Wang says, not commenting on the way Eli stiffens next to her. "Outside of that, Tong has expressed interest in helping with the rehoming process, since he's already been doing that a bit with you, and I'm confident he won't hesitate to keep us in line. Like Eli said, this is meant to be a mutually beneficial transaction: for you, for us, and for the dragons you've been taking care of all this time. We want to figure out the details with you — not as just another student employee or an outside contact, but as a partner. That position means more work for you, of course, but also more control and decision-making power. I've given you a lot of contingencies and 'we'll figure it out when we get to it,' but does that sound like a good starting point for you?"

Careful not disturb Mei, Kai reaches for his tea. Eli can hear the cages creak above them, tianlong stretching their wings or shifting in their midday naps. The humidifier hums; pipes hiss; tanks burble, plastic tubes pumping out toxins and in oxygen for the dragons lazing inside. *All dragons are at least partially aquatic,* Eli hears Kai say in his mind, a memory of leaning over tanks as Kai points at and describes each dragon, *but shuilong are the only ones who have to spend most of their adult life in or near water. Too much time on land, and they start to dry out, skin getting papery and scales flaking off. It's why you almost never find strays in urban environments — their skin is built to absorb nutrients from the water, so they're incredibly sensitive to changes in pH and chemical composition. They're literally too thin-skinned to survive the city —*

And what about us, Eli remembers wondering. What is it about people that drives them to build and live in places from which other animals would rightfully flee?

Kai's comment about being "otherwise unavailable" lodges like a splinter under Eli's skin. What does that mean? What else could it mean when Kai is sick and so stubbornly refusing help?

With a soft clink, Kai places his cup down.

"All right," he says, raising his eyes to meet Dr. Wang's. "I'll have to ask for a tour at some point so you can further explain your plans — a proper tour, I mean, and not Eli sneaking me in like some pet he's smuggling into the dorms —"

"Hey," Eli protests. "It was you sneaking animals into your dorm, not me."

"But I don't see any problems with what you've laid out," Kai finishes, ignoring him. "In terms of medical testing, I'm not comfortable with the idea of sacrificing patients for some greater good, even if it's standard practice. But they do clinical trials with experimental medicines on humans too, so if something similar was developed for dragons, with a focus on minimalizing risk relative to potential benefit — 'health related, life entrusted,' or the veterinary equivalent — I think that could be a good start. I've been doing what I can," Kai says, nodding at the surrounding clutter of tanks and cages, "and it'll be good to have proper supplies and funding."

Fond exasperation written across his face, Kai glances at Eli. "But if you want to get technical, Beida's been funding this project for a couple of weeks now."

"It's a deal?"

Forearms on the table, Kai leans in. "The start of one, yes."

They shake on it.

"Oh, don't look so pleased with yourself," Kai says, rolling his eyes at the expression on Eli's face, "we haven't done anything yet."

"Kaifei's right," Dr. Wang says, pouring herself another cup of tea. "There's paperwork to do before we can formalize things, but this is something concrete to work on — and funding committees love concrete proposals."

She takes a meditative sip, hands encircling the cup. "It's going to take a while before any kind of agreement. You know how committees are, couldn't get a damn thing done on time if their lives depended on it. Until then, I'll talk to my colleagues in veterinary medicine. They're constantly complaining about how their students could do with more practice. In any case," she says, smiling at that, "you're both smart kids — we'll figure something out, I'm sure."

"I'm not your tour guide," Kai says, shading his eyes against the sun, "You can't keep asking me to skip work to take you around Beijing."

"And yet you keep on accompanying me on these trips," Eli says. In the blinding afternoon light, his skin is burnished bronze, his legs endless in a pair of green floral shorts. A pair of oversized sunglasses covers half his face, the sight somehow ridiculous and endearing at once. "Why is that, I wonder?"

"You keep buying me things," Kai says, considering the two ice creams Eli is holding.

"It's a hot day," Eli says, handing one cone over. "Besides, I'm pulling you out of work, aren't I? It's the least I can do."

Kai rolls his eyes, but he takes the ice cream. It's sesame and already melting, and he licks cream off his fingers before it can drip further down his hand. Eli smiles at it, fond and amused, and hands Kai a napkin.

"Where to go, tour guide?"

Unlike the nearby Jingshan or Beiha parks, Ritan is one of the less ostentatious national parks, but that does not mean much in Beijing. Even less so on a day like this: still summer, but cool enough that there are a significant number of locals among the normal crowds of tourists, Beijing families cautiously venturing out into the heat for brief vacations of their own. Greying men wearing Cartier watches and T-shirts emblazoned with the names of American sports teams walk past, their powdered middle-aged wives following behind with Louis Vuitton face masks and flowered umbrellas. Once in a while, one of them glances at the sky, the clouds gathering there providing a brief reprieve from the heat.

Eli gathers their popsicle sticks when they finish, dropping them into a nearby trash bin. He's smiling to himself. It's different from the way he usually smiles out at the world, more reassurance of friendliness than a sign of actual emotion.

Eli catches Kai staring. His smile widens, and Kai looks away.

84

To distract from the flush he can feel rising, Kai asks, staring resolutely at his sneakers, "don't you have a lab you need to work at or something?"

"There are other people at the lab." Eli says. "I've taken over plenty of shifts for them before; now I'm giving them the chance to repay the favor. Besides, half of the program is about being a cultural ambassador, making connections. I'm making up for lost time."

"And you're doing that," Kai says, "by walking around parks and buying overpriced ice cream from street vendors."

"Someone has to do it," Eli says, shrugging. "Besides, the rest of them are usually either on field trips to 'important cultural sites' or out getting drunk and dancing at clubs. And well, it's not exactly like I'm into bad baijiu and girls anyways."

"Because you don't like girls."

"No," Eli says, thoughtful. "I wasn't sure I liked *anyone* actually, not in the way we're talking about at least, but it turned out I was wrong about that too. It's been interesting, these past couple of weeks. Not bad," he says, smiling as he furtively squeezes Kai's hand, once, before letting go. "Just interesting."

Interesting can mean many things, Kai knows from experience. He thinks of his high school classmate Linghu, who'd lost his scholarship and was practically disowned by his parents after he was caught kissing the school board director's son, and of all the horror stories that had percolated through the informal queer student groups at Beishida. Eli, though — Eli has college professors for parents, lives in America where there are laws and marriage rights instead of mere decriminalization. Kai knows how little these things can matter, but he can't help but hope, for Eli's sake, that his case is different.

"You know," Kai says — because even if Eli has taken his recent self-revelations in stride, this is Eli's first relationship and it is important to make this clear — "if you're still feeling your way through things, we don't have to do anything, all right? A lot of people seem to think there are things you have to do when you're doing this sort of thing. But I'm not … if any of that makes you uncomfortable, then it's not important, we don't need to do it. Normal relationships and things you're supposed to do — those don't matter. Not as much as you feeling comfortable."

"Very eloquent. What, were you planning on propositioning me?"

Kai kicks Eli in the shin, refusing to feel guilty at Eli's look of betrayal. "I'm being serious here."

"So am I. Kai, I appreciate the thought, but you don't have to worry. I'm not doing anything I don't want to do. Besides," Eli says, smiling at Kai, "I've got, what, at least fifteen centimeters on you? I'm not sure how you'd force me to do anything."

"Excuse you," Kai says, scowling up at Eli. "I can and have fought men twice your height."

"That sounds anatomically impossible, but I believe you."

Kai goes for Eli's shins again, but Eli dodges neatly out of the way. Kai scowls up at him; Eli smiles, sweet as sugar from his unfair height.

"What about you?" Eli asks as they pass a group of grandmothers practicing tai chi. "How long have you known?"

"Always, I think," Kai says with a shrug. "It feels that way, at least. The same age most people start figuring these things out, I guess — twelve, maybe, thirteen? Definitely before I finished middle school, though."

"That must have been difficult, to know so young."

"It was, but it was good, in another sense. I didn't have to go through too many years of pretending otherwise before I knew." In a way, it had been a relief figuring it out, understanding the reason his classmates' talk of breasts and women's soft skin had never resonated with him. There had been loneliness, yes, and fear at first, but there had also been the certainty of knowing.

"Does your mother know?" Eli asks.

"No," Kai says. "It was a few years after my father died, and my mother was still not well, not herself. I thought she was busy enough, between her job at the paint factory and taking care of my sister and me. There was no reason for her to know. There's no reason for her to know now."

"Do you want her to know?"

"Does it matter?"

"I think so, yes," Eli says, and his eyes are serious when he looks up from the ground, eyelashes long and outlined in golden sunlight. "Keeping all of that secret, all the time — that could be hard, sometimes. It would be for me, at least."

They can't hold hands — not here, not this publicly — but they're walking close to each other, fingers brushing more often than is coincidental. The ridiculous sunglasses sit atop Eli's hair, oversized and gaudy in the way of cheap tourist plastic. A few curls flop over his face, partially covering one eye; Kai hesitates, then reaches up and brushes them out of the way. Lets his hand linger, skin against skin.

A few children run past them on the path, and they break away, making way for them. Kai glances around, an old instinct — but no, no one has turned toward them, no one has noticed.

Eli notices, of course — Eli's always noticed, that's the whole problem — and deliberately, he reaches over and brushes his hand against Kai's. Smiles, as though he does not know how dangerous that expression is, the impossible things it does to Kai's heart.

"Hey, it looks like they're about to race," Eli says, tugging at his sleeve as he points toward the river, where several dragon boats are gathered. Bright scales are painted along the sides of the boats, and carved dragon figureheads bob in the water as if surveying the crowds. "Let's go see who'll win."

Kai glances over, sighs. "You know they're a tourist trap, don't you?"

"Well," Eli says, and it is ridiculous how bright his smile is, as if there is nowhere else he would rather be than here, the air sticky and thick around them, "I am a tourist, aren't I? I should get to enjoy it."

A breeze is blowing through the willow copses, and a cool mist billows over from the lake. The meteorologists are predicting rain, the first in three weeks, and tourists are throwing rice into the water and leaving zongzi by the statues of the Great Ones. The Dragon Kings of the Four Seas gleam in the sunlight, and at their center the Yellow Dragon shines even brighter, tall and proud in his position as mythic ancestor of them all. Kai knows the statues' polished appearance is only because of the tourists, visitors from the suburbs and Hebei come to pay their traditional respects, but he still lets himself be comforted.

"Hey, hey!" a bare-chested man says, waving at them from his stall. His English is tourist-perfected, the choppy salesperson's dialect of selling gaudy plastic to jet-lagged foreigners. There's a small cage in his hand, several dozen more on a table inside the stall, a dragon in each — dilong, the small scavengers sold to children at summer fairs alongside turtles and goldfish. "Forty dollars! Take back, nice gift!"

Eli glances at Kai, who only shrugs.

"And how," Eli asks in perfect Mandarin as he turns to the salesman, "would I take these back on the plane, exactly?"

"You speak Chinese?"

"I do," Eli says. "I mean, at the least, I believe I do? Kai? What are your thoughts?"

Kai cocks his head to one side, pretends to consider the issue seriously. "Now that I think about it, I think you do."

"Not a lot of foreigners can do it," the salesman says, walking toward them. "How about that then? Special discount, 200 renminbi. Bring one home cheap for being so talented? Sold a pair off to a nice family in Australia — they went back with little presents for their children. Not lying, you can ask other people — lots of tourists come here, bring back pets for their friends."

"Thanks," Eli says, "but I'll pass for now."

"How about something else then, yeah? You go home, and you take something for your family or friends, yeah? You have a girlfriend? We can do her name in calligraphy, real nice too, take it home for her. Pretty thing for a pretty girl, yeah?"

"Sorry," Kai says, "but I don't think either of us are interested."

"How 'bout Mom, then?" The man is hopping after them now, his smile wet and yellow. "We sell necklaces, purses — genuine leather, good stuff. Dragon skin too if you want something special, powdered scale cream that'll do wonders for dry skin —"

Kai moves without thinking. One moment, Kai's watching a street vendor attempting to hawk goods to his amused American target; the next he's rushing the man, face so close he can smell the tobacco on the vendor's breath.

"I told you," Kai says, hands clenching into fists at his sides, "we aren't interested."

The man is a full head taller than him, but Kai doesn't care. If the vendor says a single word — if he tries to say anything, if he tries to touch him —

"Kai?"

Kai takes a deep breath, forces himself to walk away. Behind him, he can hear Eli apologizing to the vendor before hurrying after him. It only takes Eli a few strides to catch up.

"You didn't have to do that. It wasn't real, you know."

"Of course it wasn't," Kai says. "No one would sell dragon skin for that price. He was still trying to pass it off, though." And people would have bought it; that was the issue. Not all of them, but the more foolish or less demanding of them, those stupid enough to believe luxury could be bought on the streets or otherwise willing to settle for secondhand imitations of luxury, because there was a market for this, wasn't there? No matter how illegal, no matter how cruel, there would always be a market for it —

Eli's hand is hesitant as it brushes against his, his voice even more so. "Kai?"

89

He forces the anger down, forces himself to be steady when he speaks. "That man," Kai says, and he's proud of how calm his voice is, "didn't know the first thing about dragons or taking care of them, and he thinks he can sell them off to tourists." At the temple, the monks had told stories of the first emperor, how Heaven saw his noble deeds and so turned him into a dragon on his death. For centuries, it was said the people of his nation were the children of dragons, the dragons themselves the reincarnations of wise men and children yet to be born.

And now here they were. A nation ready to skin and sell its children for money.

"It's not all their fault, you know," Eli says as they make their way back to the main path. "A lot of these people, they're poor, they have families, they're desperate and they don't know what to do. They just want to make money."

"Lots of people are poor. That doesn't make them do anything."

"Kai, you can't expect everyone to be an activist."

"Can't I?"

Eli says nothing, but rather than vindication, all Kai feels is hollowness. They're still walking together, but there's a distinct distance between them now, no easy banter or covert attempts at touching.

It had been such a good day before this.

"C'mon," Eli says, already striding toward the next tourist attraction, a bronze bust staring past the flash of smartphone cameras. He smiles at Kai, a simultaneous peace offering and silent entreaty. "I need to get my cultural ambassador hours in. Tell me the history of this statue, tour guide?"

When the rain comes, Kai is walking home, a plastic bag of cup noodles and prepackaged pineapple buns in one hand.

Even as he curses and runs for cover, plastic bag held over his head a paltry cover, there's a part of him that relishes it — the waterlogged squeak of his sneakers, the drag of soaked clothes against skin, the way the rain transforms the world into an impressionistic canvas of streaking watercolors. The itch in his lungs for once quiet, drowned by the roar of the rain. If he closes his eyes, Kai can almost imagine he is breathing in more water than air, suspended underwater for precious seconds stolen out of time.

It doesn't last long. The rain comes down hard and fast, tearing the leaves off trees and battering the dusty streets to a muddy froth, and then it is over, hot sun burning away the raindrops almost before they finish falling.

Standing beneath the awning of a medicine shop with his hair plastered to his forehead and heart still thumping from the sprint to shelter, Kai catches his breath. Though the afternoon sun shines as harshly as ever, in the wake of the rain there's a difference to the air. A clarity, if only temporary.

It takes four knocks before Kai answers the door, and when he does, his face is drawn. His eyes say *go away*.

"Hi," Eli says. "Mr. Lin told me you would be here. Can I come in?"

After a pause, Kai nods.

Eli takes his shoes off, keeping his eyes on Kai all the while.

"Kai?" he asks gently. "Are you all right?"

In response, Kai points at a cloth-covered tank. Eli squats down, lifts the fabric from the tank. As the whirring of the fan cuts through the silence, the cloth flutters in the breeze, settling against the glass once more.

"Today," Kai says, not looking at the dragons. They're so thin it hurts to look at them, skin dull and sagging over protruding bones. Patches of dried-out scales cluster like grey ashes, blood welling up from where scales have cracked or fallen off. "All today."

"Kai? Are you —"

"There are so *many* of them," Kai says, wearily resting his head in his hands. "I know there always are, all over the city. I see them all the time, and it's fine, it's all right most of the time, but this — right here, I swear to God —" Kai takes a breath, and then shakes his head. "I'm all right," he says finally. "It's fine. I'm fine."

Eli reaches for Kai's hand; when Kai does not move away, Eli takes it and holds it for a long while.

The sun is not yet up when Eli wakes, but it doesn't matter; though his head aches with sleep deprivation, the prospect of more dreams is enough to keep his eyes open. Even so, visions of flickering red linger. There had been fire in every direction, ceiling beams crashing down in bursts of cinders as Eli searched for Kai or Mei or some sign of an exit. Trapped in their cages, the dragons had screamed and screamed, but when Eli reached out to free them the cages had stretched further into the depths of the blaze, the familiar space of Kai's apartment warping into a dizzying kaleidoscope of disjointed hallways. And where was Kai? Where could he have gone and how could Eli have lost him? How was he supposed to find him now with the flames rising higher and the crackle of burnt and falling wood all around them —

It's psychosomatic, but Eli thinks he can taste smoke when he inhales.

He stumbles into the bathroom, bare feet slapping faintly against the tiles. Standing in front of the sink with his eyes closed, he splashes cold water over his face. When he finally opens his eyes, the water from his hair dripping down his forehead, he sees the blood on the sink.

Eli stares. Tries to imagine that it is something else — some trick of the light, a splotch of paint, or the result of a bite from Mei or another of Kai's endless charges — but it is no use. The red remains, stark and half-dried, and Eli can't help thinking *stage progression* and *lung tissue* and *symptomatic*.

Clutching the edges of the sink, he closes his eyes, counts to one, two, three. When he opens his eyes, the blood is still there.

Outside, on the balcony, Eli studies the view before him. There's not much to see — Kai's apartment faces out onto a row of grey apartment units, window blinds closed and occupants silent at this early hour. It is already a muggy, grey day, the way so many days seem to be in Beijing, but it is peaceful. For that Eli is grateful.

Eli takes a deep, slow breath, then straightens. Smooths his hair, rubs his hands to still their trembling. Kai's apartment is on the eighth floor of thirteen, and below, a bald man loiters by the trash collection — Eli wonders if he's maybe seen him before. Is he one of the loudmouthed old men who linger at the entrance to Mr. Lin's shop? But then he is gone, and the street is empty again.

The sun, coming up, paints the sky in hazy pink.

Inside, Kai is in the same position in which Eli had left him, still asleep. He curls in on himself, as if protecting the rise and fall of breath in his chest. Deprived of his anger, Kai looks so small and so tired. In the dawning light, his skin is the color of washed-out moonlight, the hairs on the back of his neck gossamer strands, almost glowing.

Then, in this sleepy pre-dawn interlude, Eli is wrenched by an anger so violent it startles him. Fuck no, this is *wrong*. Kai is twenty-one — he should be out with friends or training with experts on wildlife rescue, not here, cooped up in an apartment with only piecemeal resources and a ticking timer on his future. But the anger subsides, leaving in its wake a desolate powerlessness. *But what can be done?*

Something, he thinks. He couldn't be completely helpless. He wouldn't be. There had to be something he could do to help.

When Eli's grandmother died, no one had expected it. Oh, they'd prepared for it, in the way people prepared for retirement or power outages — something they knew would happen, yes. But even just before it happened, the prospect of his grandmother's death seemed so firmly rooted to an unknown future as to be unreal. His grandmother had been sick for so long in a low-grade, chronic way that the disease had come to feel like stability, oxygen tanks and ventilation masks another background detail of video calls. She was sick, but she still made her own meals and watered her garden daily, still read the news each morning and took blurry photos of stray cats. She still engaged in the small, ordinary tasks that make up a life.

And then she had died. No ambulance called, no sharp turn in health or protracted hospice stay — his grandmother had simply gone to bed one evening and did not rise in the morning. Her cats' wailing had been what finally alerted the neighbors. If his grandmother had lived alone or been a little less fond of her routines, how long would it have taken someone to notice, how long would she have laid there, cold and unmoving, before her landlord or a neighbor finally thought to check in?

On the bed, Kai shifts in his sleep, murmuring something indecipherable before falling still once more. Gently, so as not to wake him, Eli brushes the hair from Kai's forehead, fingers lingering when Kai doesn't stir.

Something. There must be something — anything — he could do, some combination of the right words and care that will compel Kai to accept his help. But as the sun rises in the sky and Kai remains soundly asleep, Eli can only sit there, hands clenched in the bedsheets.

5

Sunday morning. Hazy sunlight filters in through dusty glass as a new fan steadily *click-click-clicks* in one corner, interrupted only by the intermittent splash or rustle from the dragons in their tanks and cages. As he waits for the kettle to boil, Eli presses a cheek against the cool glass of the kitchen window and watches Beijing blur below. A few feet away, Kai sits on his bed, pillows propped behind his back. Mei is curled catlike in his lap, occasionally stretching her neck as something catches her attention.

There is, Eli has learned over time, a metric to the kind of kindness Kai will accept. Offer money, a meal at the noodle shop across from the lab, a water bottle from the pack of Nongfu Spring Dr. Wang keeps stocked in the break room for students, and Kai will bristle, draw back in a cold silence of affronted pride and stubborn self-sufficiency. Offer him supplies or water filters to help him take care of the dragons, however, and Kai will complain, but he will take them. Eli tries not to exploit this too much, but on a day like this, when the heat wraps around them like a blanket and Kai is so very quiet, he is glad that his flimsy excuse about optimal environmental conditions had been enough to let Kai accept the offered humidifier and new fans with relative equanimity. Even so, it's hot, the kind of day that Eli has always associated with childhood — the dog days of summer, the last lazy afternoons before real life and school intrude again. In recent years, the summers have come earlier and lasted longer, so that instead of a few days of scorching heat it feels like Eli spends half of

August hiding inside. And that's in New England with air conditioning in his dorm — Eli can't imagine how Kai has spent months in Beijing with only a cheap box fan for comfort. *Willpower*, Kai would probably say, one of those self-satisfied answers that always make Eli a little sad. Kai shouldn't have to subsist on willpower, not when streets away condos are empty and unused.

Closing the curtains, he turns to Kai.

"Weather says it's going to rain soon," Eli says, sitting next to him. "Things might get a little better then."

"They keep saying that," Kai says. "But it never happens. It's like they think if they keep repeating it, it'll finally rain."

"It has to rain some time. This weather can't last forever."

"Mm," Kai says, neither agreement nor disagreement. Strands of hair stick to his forehead and his skin is faintly red, a flush Eli knows has only partially to do with the heat. Eli wants to lean over and smooth away the furrow between his brows, but he's unsure how welcome the gesture would be.

In their cages and tanks, the dragons are dozing, ribs pressing in and out of sharpness with slow breaths. Eli pours tea for himself and Kai, nudging a cup toward Kai until he takes it and drinks.

"You know the story of Nezha, don't you?"

"I think there was a cartoon version we watched in Chinese school once," Eli says, putting the teapot on the kitchen table. "It was a long time ago though. Why?"

"It's a pretty popular story," Kai says. He reaches down to pet Mei, who is assiduously chewing on the hem of his T-shirt. "It's a folk story," Kai says. "Nezha was a folk hero, way, way back. Born into a royal family. His mother initially gives birth to a giant ball of flesh but Nezha comes out perfectly fine, apart from being able to walk from infancy. But that's folk heroes for you. Grows up a mostly normal kid, except for the flying and other supernatural powers.

"A few years go by, and there's a major drought. Crops are dying, the price of food is going up, people are starving. So they decide to hold a bunch of sacrifices to the dragon king, Ao Guang — this was back when there was less of a divide between humans and gods. And Ao Guang, because he's been king for a long time and he's used to getting what he wants, demands the people give him children to eat if they want it to rain. They try giving him rice, but it won't do — he wants soft child meat, and he's not the type to be satisfied when people don't give him what he wants. So, instead of waiting for his subjects to change their minds, he gets one of his lackeys to kidnap some kids for dinner. They're Nezha's friends, though, and of course when Nezha finds out, he's not happy. And, being the supernatural semi-demigod child he is, he decides to fight the East Dragon King."

"Pretty understandable," Eli says. He reaches for Kai's hand, careful not to disturb Kai's other hand as it strokes Mei's smooth neck, and takes it in his own. Kai's palms are dry and work-worn, but he has long, elegant fingers. *Piano fingers*, his mother would have called them. "He sounds kind of unreasonable, this dragon king."

"He was a king," Kai says, shifting away so that Eli has to stretch to reach him. "It's what they do. If you've ever seen any of the Sun Wukong adaptations, there are a couple of dragon kings in those stories too, and they're just as good at razing cities as the old European firebreathers were, just more bureaucratic about their destruction.

"Anyway, Nezha goes out to fight the Dragon King's troops. It's a long fight. Nezha's this tiny kid flying around on his flaming wheels and thrashing the dragon generals with his magic sash. But at the end of it, he wins — no children get eaten, the people are freed from the tyranny of their old king, et cetera."

"And they all lived happily ever."

"Basically," Kai says. "There's a part later on when all the dragon kings get angry and Nezha has to kill himself to stop a mass genocide, but then he comes back later, so it's fine."

Eli isn't sure how to respond. "That," he settles on, "is a generous definition of fine."

On Kai's lap, Mei stands, arching her back in a stretch as she pads over to curl up with her flank pressed against his leg. Kai absently runs a hand down her spine, and Mei closes her eyes, settling into the sheets.

"So what?" Eli asks as he reaches over, gently scratching the area behind Mei's frill; she leans into the touch, rumbling against his fingers. "You think we should start sacrificing children again if we want it to rain?"

"Of course not," Kai says, rolling his eyes. He stands up and makes his way over to the lines of tanks. Frowns as he leans down to adjust several knobs, fingers tapping over the salinity dials before shifting them up. "It's just a story; you're not meant to take it seriously."

"Ah. The cultural ambassador thing, then."

"Exactly," Kai says, adjusting the settings on the last tank. "Can't have you go back to America like we didn't teach you a thing about the local culture." Shoulder bumping against Eli's, Kai reclaims his spot on the bed, settling his head against the pillows. Eli hesitates, then moves closer so Kai's head is resting on his shoulder. Kai doesn't say anything, and Eli dares to put a hand on his head, gently brush Kai's bangs from his eyes. "Anyway," Kai says, closing his eyes. "It was just a story."

It hadn't sounded like just a story, Eli thinks. Old, hard gods and the price of water and kingdoms that would sacrifice their children for the hope of another day — it's a familiar story, cousin to a litany of other stories across other mythologies. An archetypal legend, but no less true for its familiarity.

Kai is warm against him, too hot skin almost unpleasant in the sticky heat, but Eli doesn't move. He studies the minute changes of expression across Kai's face, the spray of red, almost freckle-like dots across one wrist.

"It'll rain soon," Eli says, stroking Kai's inner wrist. Blue-green veins stand out against thin skin and Kai's pulse is fast beneath Eli's fingers, the sharp staccato beat of raindrops against a windowpane. "It will."

It's past sunset when the first bettors gather, a scraggly group of old standbys and swaggering newcomers ready to test their luck. All together, they total barely a dozen including spectators, not quite enough to justify the need for a referee. But midseason is always a slow time for dragon fights. Attendance will pick up toward the end of the season, Kai knows, when the points get tallied and the final competitors are squared away. Until then, it is a matter of sustaining interest. Mr. Lin is in the back of the shop, moving in a new shipment of tubes and aquarium filters, and so Kai sits at the counter, only half paying attention as he takes names and bets from the men gathered.

It's one of the rare nights when Eli is not there, having gone to some formal dinner or gala with attendance so mandatory even he could not escape it. He had been apologetic when he left, and even as Kai assured him that it was fine, that he could survive a night alone, he had been privately grateful. As much as Kai appreciates Eli's company, there is something oddly exhausting about being around him. Kai is technically younger by about a year, but he always feels so much older than Eli, with his unbridled earnestness and wholehearted belief in the ability of people to change. It's a relief, sometimes, after an afternoon or evening with Eli, to go home or to Mr. Lin's and let all his cynicism breathe once again.

Perhaps that says something about who he is as a person, Kai muses as he pulls his pencils out of his bag, laying them out in front of him. Perhaps it doesn't. How much does his inherent goodness matter when he's one person in a country of billions?

He leans his elbows on the counter, staring out at landscape before him. It's the same view he's seen every night at Mr. Lin's — the lines of old shops behind them, the grey, thick air above. There's something, though, in the way the lights flicker tonight, in the way they cast long shadows fluttering across the ground and blurring everything into impressionist streaks — it's a thickness to the air that isn't quite smog or heat or the ever-present scent of grease. Kai frowns, flipping his pencil between his fingers as he compares the sketch against his view of the shops before him, trying to tease out the invisible quality of the space. Perhaps if he darkened a line here, pressed a little harder as he shaded there, he could capture it.

His first year of college, Kai had taken an art class, partially out of curiosity, partially to stop his friends from telling him how much he ought to take one. It had been much what he'd expected — his classmates a mix of cooler-than-thou design students and politicians' children who thought themselves artistic — but some of the exercises had been useful and he had liked the professor, a wiry, competent woman with calloused sculptor's hands and a refreshing lack of tolerance for bullshit. It's Professor Jing he thinks of as he smudges the charcoal along one sketched brick wall to better illuminate the fuzzy halos of the streetlamps. "Your art is technically proficient," she had told him the last time they met, sipping tea in her office two weeks before the constant heat under his skin led Kai to finally visit the student health center. "It always has been — even as a first-year, your grasp of anatomy and attention to detail were impressive. But there's something I can't help but feel is missing, there's something you're holding back. Your work is good, Kaifei, but it's static, neat. It's pretty, but it's not alive yet."

Kai wonders idly, his sketched scene blooming out before him, what Professor Jing would think if she saw what he was doing now, the piles of sketches cluttering his table, the canvases lining his walls. He wonders what his mother would say. If she saw his art and knew anything of what it meant.

He had tried to call her the other morning. He had been meaning to for a while. Despite whatever Eli might think on the subject, Kai is not stupid; he knows how shaolong progresses, the inevitabile worsening symptoms. In stage four and late stage three, patients are usually housebound, toxin-induced coughing fits strong enough to cause fainting and heart palpitations. Compared to those cases, Kai has been lucky, symptoms primarily contained to shortness of breath and coughing more like asthma or allergies than shaolong. He can still walk upstairs and lift boxes with relative ease, and if he occasionally spits blood, he can treat it at home instead of surrendering to an interminable hospital stay. Kai is stable, unpleasant as that stability is. But he knows it cannot last.

And Eli had been right on another thing too: his mother deserves to know. However he might have justified it at the beginning, he knows it isn't altruism that keeps him from telling her. It's cowardice.

At the beginning of the summer, his old phone broke. Fell off his bed at an angle that touchscreens were not built to withstand, a lattice of cracks spidering across the glass. It'd been an accident, but a convenient one, the perfect excuse to give to his mother and any college friends determined to ask why he wasn't keeping in touch. Even after he got a replacement, a blocky but functional Huawei bought secondhand, Kai conveniently forgot to give his new number to others. Later, he reasoned. When he was feeling steadier, more like himself.

A few days ago, for the first time in months, Kai had called his mother. Punched in the familiar numbers in his new phone, and the call had been sent to voicemail, his mother's tired but friendly voice telling him that she was busy but that he should leave a message. She would answer back as soon as she could.

Of course. His mother never answered her phone while she was at work.

He hadn't left a message. He hadn't tried again.

Kai frowns, tilting his head to view the drawing from different forty-five-degree angles, but the threads guiding him forward have vanished, the whisper that this line went there and that shape there now silent. It's all right, though. He has the gist of it down, the bones of what he wants to create on this page; it's only a matter of cleaning things up, figuring out where to go from there.

There's a mood Kai gets into when he draws, a mood in which the whole world seems to fade away. It doesn't last, and sometimes the art isn't even good, but it's always welcome. This mood is a part of why, he supposes, he's been so productive this summer. Emerging from it is always a shock, and here, at Mr. Lin's, even more so, with its noise and lights and sweat all crammed together, condensed into a panoply of sheer humanity.

Placing his sketchpad under the counter, Kai stands and rubs his hands over his eyes. He walks outside, rolling his shoulders to ease the stiffness from sitting so long. Staring out at the crowd, he lets himself adjust. Slowly, the world comes back to him: swatches of color coalesce into shapes, faces; the roaring white noise separating into voices, words emerging out of the noise.

"Jiayou, jiayou, c'mon, little closer now, by the fucking neck —"

"To the left, that's it, come on, that's it, you've got him —"

"Motherfucker — son of a bitch, fucking hell, useless piece of shit —"

This last invective is from one of the newer attendees, a man Kai has seen once or twice before — always on the sidelines of matches, betting and watching the outcomes. He's drunk, obvious from the sloppy imprecision of his movements, the redness of his face as he stamps his feet, cursing at the dragon cowering in front of him. As Kai watches, the man grabs the dragon by the skin of its neck, forcing it to its feet. The dragon squeals, claws scrabbling against the ground as it struggles against the hold. "Yes, come on now you piece of shit, get the fuck up and fight —"

"Excuse me," Kai says, voice loud as he walks toward the man, "I'm going to have to ask you to stop now."

The man turns, raising bloodshot eyes to Kai. He's a tall, burly man, forearms tattooed, with the kind of muscle rarely seen outside of bodybuilding magazines and pornography.

"What?" he asks. His tone matches his appearance: drunk with an incredulous edge. "And who the fuck are you?"

"I work here," Kai says. "And, as acting referee until Lin returns, I'm telling you that unless you have another dragon here, you're out. We follow regulation practices for elimination — your dragon can't or doesn't want to fight, so it's the other trainer's win. We're not in the business of snuff fights."

"Yeah?" There's amusement on his face now, easy contempt as the man sneers at him. It's a familiar expression, one Kai knows well from the faces of a hundred schoolyard bullies, and the derisive police officers who had written up his friends for indecent exposure for kissing in public. "And what do you expect us to do instead, parade these things around like some sort of breed exhibition?"

If Kai were younger, the taunt might have landed. As it is, Kai squares his shoulders and maintains eye contact. "As acting referee, it is my job to tell you what you can do. And what I'm telling you is that you've had your chance for the night and lost. Unless you want to deal with the consequences of blatant rule violation, that means you're done for tonight. That's all it is."

"What, all this fighting bother you?" The man leans in, close enough that Kai can almost taste the alcohol on his breath. "Too much for your little heart, princess? Oh, but this," he says, sending another contemptuous kick at the dragon, who squeals as she curls away, "this ain't nothing — just a little encouragement. Goddamn animals, you can't get them to do nothing without a push. Don't worry though, sweetheart — I won't let anything *too* bad happen."

104

He smirks, straightening as he turns back to the ring.

"I said," Kai says, stepping into the man's path, "you're going to stop, or you're going to leave."

The man stares at him, bristling with anger and irritation. Kai stares back, refusing to look away, to be in any way cowed.

The man glances back at his friends, who shrug; well, so what? Some of them are smiling, not even bothering to conceal their amusement. Kai knows what he looks like from the outside, his short but wiry college student physique against this man with the shoulders of a brawler and the eyes of a man used to getting his way. Kai doesn't flinch as he holds the man's gaze.

The man scowls. By his sides, his fists clench tight.

Do it. Kai is surprised by the viciousness of the thought, the strength of his desire for the man to hit him or say something, anything, any excuse for him to hit back —

"Hey! You harassing my staff?"

It's Mr. Lin, flip flops flapping over hard gravel and hands in the pockets of baggy cargo shorts as he stalks over, but no less imposing for that.

"Well?" Mr. Lin asks, arching an eyebrow as he stops in front of the two of them. "The fuck's going on here?"

"Lin da-ge," the man says, and though his words are still slurred, his voice is calmer now, almost saccharine in its reasonability. "I'm here trying to get my dragons up and through this round, and then this kid tells me he's in charge of this place and I need to stop. And I tell him to piss off, but he keeps going, telling me what I'm supposed to do with my own dragons. The nerve of it, the goddamn presumption of the fucking kids today —"

"Enough," Mr. Lin cuts in, decisively enough that the man actually stops. "I'll take care of that later," he says, giving Kai a curt nod. "But right now ..." Mr. Lin's eyes scan the scene before him, level, assessing. Kai can read the conclusions forming as clearly as if he was speaking aloud: the scars patterned over the prominent rib cage, the thin line of scratches down legs and tail — none of them particularly serious, critical points covered by the traditional protective leather, but still painful irritants sure to fester and scar without proper care. The dull, dry look of blue scales, the ragged, cut wings — not technically a legal practice anymore, but not uncommon. Mr. Lin turns again, now evaluating the stranger before them: the bloodshot eyes, the scent of alcohol coming off him in waves.

"Kai's right," he says, voice low but controlled. "You treat your dragons like that, we don't want you here. Sober up or get out."

The man looks ready to argue, but Mr. Lin matches his glare with his own flat gaze, the one he's honed on scores of hapless employees and recalcitrant dragons. The man is drunk and angry, but he's not blind.

"We're closing early," Kai says, smile all teeth. "Have a good night."

"Kai," Mr. Lin says, turning once the man is a hunched silhouette retreating into the darkness. His voice is a deliberate calm that can only mean trouble. "I'd ask for an explanation, but I'm not sure there is one, is there?"

"Then there's no point in trying to give one, is there?" Kai asks, equally rhetorical. "He was a jackass, I called him out on it. He deserved it."

"I'm sure he did. But when this happens, you come and tell me — you don't go picking fights with strangers. Old man in heaven, Kai, you've done this before, you know how to deal with drunks —"

"We should have taken the dragon," Kai says, still watching the retreating form of the drunk man's back. "He's just going to find another ring after this."

"And what? You think that'll help, that he won't just get another dragon if we did? That you'll what — kidnap every animal or kid that looks vaguely mistreated, and that'll do it? End all the fucking injustice in the world, happily ever after and no more war ever again?"

"Maybe," Kai says. "Maybe it would help, at least." He is aware, vaguely, that he should apologize, try in some way to defuse the stupidity of talking back to the man who controls his paycheck, but he can't find in it himself to care.

"Go home, Kai," Mr. Lin says finally, his words controlled as he turns away. "You're scaring off the other customers."

Eli's on his laptop, looking through the pages of foreign exchange programs, when his phone buzzes. He blinks at his phone, surprised, and then sees the name on the screen. The guilt rushes in: his mother. Of course.

"Hi, Mom," he says, hoping his smile doesn't look too sheepish as he adjusts the screen.

"Hello to you too, Eli," his mother says, settling in her seat. "It's been a while, hasn't it? Thought you might have forgotten about me, you know."

He winces. "Sorry. Things have been busy."

"Good busy, I hope?"

Eli smiles, hoping the expression isn't too strained. "For the most part, yeah."

His mother says nothing, lips pressed as she watches him. "As long as you're having fun."

"I am. Not too much fun, though. Don't worry."

"Oh, so long as it's a reasonable amount of fun, then," his mother says, smiling as she leans back. "Speaking of which, Xiang ah-yi's daughter is having a baby shower — you remember Rebecca, right? She used to boss you around all the time when you were little, made you carry her books and play dress up with her. And now here she is, married and a baby soon too! I was going to buy her something practical, a monitor maybe, but then I saw these dinosaur onesies on Amazon, and now I can't decide."

"Don't babies grow really fast?" Eli asks, leaning back against his headboard. "Maybe a stuffed animal or toy, if you wanted something cute that'll last longer?"

His mother hums, the low, noncommittal noise that means she's taking an idea under consideration. "The shower's not for a couple weeks, so I have plenty of time to agonize over it. Speaking of change, I've been thinking of getting someone to repaint some of the house — it's been a while, you know? Now that you're leaving, it would be nice to make the place look a little newer. I'll send you links to the swatches. I know photos are terrible for color quality, but I was thinking either a light blue or green, if you had any preferences?"

"Either's okay," Eli says. "I'm sure it'll look fine."

"Are you sure? It is your bedroom, after all, and it wouldn't be any trouble to send you the colors ..."

"It's fine, Mom. Honest. Like you said, it's not like I'll be spending much time there in the future. You could rent out the room if you want to, actually feed those grad students you always complain about."

His mother frowns, the tight line of her lips signaling true disapproval, but she lets it go. "I'll send you the links any-way — I don't want any future complaints that I did this without asking."

Eli nods as she continues talking — the house, her students, news from his high school friends and his father's family. In his mind, snippets from medical papers and web-pages echo, whispers clamoring for attention: *before stage four progression, marked primarily by moderate-to-severe lung damage and fatigue associated with everyday activities, patients often experience prolonged coughing fits and increased shortness of breath ... toxicity generally confined to respiratory cells, but damage to subcutaneous tissue is also observed, sometimes leading to ... though relative stability can be achieved in early stages, if allowed to progress, then ...*

"Eli," his mother calls, and the sharpness of her voice snaps Eli's attention back to his computer. She's frowning, adjusting her phone. "Sweetheart, is everything all right?"

"What?" he asks. "Of course it is — why wouldn't it be? Sorry," he says, attempting to project reassurance with his smile, "it's just — I guess I'm a little distracted tonight."

"Elijah," his mother says, and oh, that is her mothering tone now, the one she reserves for moments of particular stupidity. "Don't lie to me. Even if I didn't spend all my time around people who do it for a living, I'm your mother; I can tell when you're keeping something from me. Something's bothering you. What is it, Eli?"

Eli considers denying it, but he knows it's no use hiding the truth — his mother, once on a mission, is ruthless the way only a professional prosecutor can be.

"Have you ever known someone," he says, "someone who was smart and talented who, for whatever reason, was in trouble and wouldn't take your help?"

"This is a friend of yours, from Beida?"

"From the lab, yeah." Kai isn't technically part of the lab, but it's close enough to the truth that he doesn't think she should be able to pick up on it.

"Your grandmother," she says. "Your father. You, sometimes. Half my family, really; sometimes I wonder if it's something genetic or if it's something about me that attracts these types of people."

"Mom —"

"It's not a criticism. I love you, Eli. But you're smart and you're stubborn, and you're used to that being enough. If you have a problem, you'd much rather muddle through it on your own than ask for help. But now you're on the other side of the problem, and it's terrible because you want to help, you want to fix this, but they won't let you."

His mother smiles, and there's something resigned in it, the same, familiar expression that never failed to make Eli feel guilty. "But you want to help them — him? — then. This friend."

Eli nods. "Him. And yeah, I do."

"And he won't let you?"

"Yeah," he says. "And I understand it on one level, but on the other, it's so frustrating. It wouldn't be anything that big, on my side, but he still won't take my help — it's so *stupid*, Mom, there's no part of it that makes sense from any angle. It's like he's being stubborn for the sake of being stubborn."

"Oh, believe me," his mother says, smiling through the screen, "I understand that, baobei. Who went on a Little League strike because his coach wouldn't let him bring his Nintendo DS to practice?"

"*Mom.*"

"Joking, baobei, just joking. You haven't changed much since then. Still so serious about everything."

"Things *are* serious this time, Mom."

"I'm not saying they aren't." Gratifyingly, his mother seems to mean it, her frown contemplative as she tilts her head to one side, considering the options. "I'm only saying, Eli, that I've done this before, and so I know how hard it can be. Some people ..." She stops, bites her lip in thought. "You should try talking to him. Be logical about it, honest. You're smart, sweetheart; I'm sure he would listen to you."

"And if he doesn't want to listen?"

He knows what she's thinking about, because his mind is on the same thing. The phone calls stretching into the night, the hushed arguments and, eventually, the begging. His grandmother's responses, offered with a crispness unsuited to someone with a terminal illness, *I'm sorry, but I can't. This is my home, and I can't leave.* The dull acceptance, almost relief, when it finally happened, Eli away at college and staring at his mother's grainy image on his laptop as she told him the news —

"Then you try again," his mother says, and over the fuzzy connection he can't tell if it's simply him projecting or not, but her voice sounds stronger, more decided. "You have to give them the right to decide, of course — it's still their decision in the end. But you have the right to try too, Eli. That's your right, baobei. You have to try."

"Why, exactly, are we here again?" Kai asks, expression nearly as mutinous as clouds above them.

Eli takes a moment before answering, taking in the day around him. The Qixi Festival means that couples swarm the walkways around them, holding hands and smiling adoringly at each other in front of unsmiling monuments. Pink lanterns hang from trees for the holiday, swaying slightly in the breeze coming off Kunming Lake. A tour boat glides past, gilt and green dragon snarling from the prow and dwarfing the rented rowboats.

"Because it's a lovely day," Eli says, as the scent of fried food and sugar wafts through the air. "And because it'll be fun? Also Dr. Wang all but forced us to go to this play, and you wouldn't be so awful as to leave me alone with my lab mates."

"I was certainly tempted," Kai mutters, hands in his pockets as they weave their way past a pair of giggling teenaged lovebirds. "I don't know why she's insisting in the first place — Qixi's not culturally important, it's an excuse for companies to sell chocolate and roses to high school kids and middle-aged businessmen."

"Hm," Eli says, resisting the urge to buy a flower from a nearby street vendor solely to see Kai's reaction. "High school kids I can understand, but middle-aged businessmen?"

"They have to make up for the emotional neglect somehow, don't they?"

"Eli, Kaifei!" Dr. Wang says, smiling as they approach her spot beneath the willow trees. Beside her, Mr. Lin looks almost as unimpressed as Kai by the festivities around them. "So glad to see you here!"

"Hi, Dr. Wang, Mr. Lin," Eli says. Kai nods a greeting to both his boss and Dr. Wang. "Where's everyone else?"

"Oh, them? They'll be here in an hour or so — I told them to come a little later, closer to the start of the Cowherd and the Weaver Girl, but I wanted to talk to you before that. The two of you, to be more accurate. I'm so glad you could get Kai out here as well. We got the results today. From the board meeting, about funding a program for studying dragons."

"Oh?" Eli says, partially because Dr. Wang seems to expect it and partially because he is surprised. Given all of Dr. Wang's warnings about academic bureaucracy, he had expected the process to take much longer. "What did they say?"

"What I expected," Dr. Wang says, leaning back against the tree. "That the project was a long shot, but given the number of departments expressing interest they were approving it. As long as I don't mind sharing responsibility with other professors. I can't complain about that. In any case," she says, nodding at Kai, "Beida is still deliberating on how much funding they're willing to give, but they're giving us a provisional grant so we can start a scaled-down version of the project. It'll take some strategic budgeting, but with help from the veterinary schools we can house fifteen to twenty dragons, maybe more if they're small. The money should last us until spring, when the committee will review our results and decide whether to extend funding for a three- or five-year-long project."

"They'll give you all that?"

"Well," Dr. Wang says, crossing her arms across her chest, "I would have preferred if they gave us the three or five years upfront, as those are the kinds of time scales you need to produce substantial results. Still, a year's not bad. At the very least, the fact that the university is giving us money instead of deliberating the issue for another five or six meetings shows that they think the idea has merit. We just need to do our job properly and make sure that opinion doesn't change."

"That's fantastic news," Eli says. In terms of medical research, Dr. Wang is right that a year's time means very little — clinical trials alone can take six years, and that's after all the work of discovering and developing a drug has been done. But a year's funding means a year that Kai doesn't have to wash cloth bandages between uses or hoard popsicle sticks and disposable chopsticks for makeshift splints, a year in which people with resources and real professional training can care for the dragons crowding Kai's apartment. And sure, it would be only fifteen or twenty dragons at a time, but with dragons transitioning out of the program as they recover, how many would that be over time? After weeks of swabbing anti-septic over cuts and rubbing burning cream on blistered scales, it's dizzying to think that this is happening, that the university has heard their scrabbled-together plans and is agreeing to make them real. Eli had hoped, of course, but those hopes had been faint.

He glances over at Kai. Asking Beida had been Eli's idea technically, but it had always felt like it belonged to Kai — his cause and his dragons. Kai is still, his face wan. If Eli is dazed by Dr. Wang's news, Kai looks like someone has kicked the ground out from under him. Kai, who lives so simply and quietly as to nearly disappear; Kai, who's cut off contact with his family and friends, who avoids doctors and ignores the needs of his own body, whose only true tether to the here and now are his dragons.

Without that tether, familiar and steady, what does Kai have keeping him moored?

"Kai?"

"I'll be right back," Kai says, and then he's gone, disap-peared into the crowd.

Kai walks quickly and the park is teeming with people, but it isn't difficult for Eli to spot him, a small, lone figure sitting at the edge of the man-made lake. With every step toward Kai, Eli is careful not to startle, not to broadcast his presence. "Are you all right?" he asks.

"Why are you here," Kai mutters. His eyes are half-closed, and he's leaning forward, arms wrapped tight around his knees.

A dozen potential answers race through Eli's mind, movie-perfect declarations of loyalty and loneliness. *I couldn't just leave — you looked like you —*

"I kind of had to find you," he says. "I couldn't let you run away, after going to all the trouble of getting you here."

It's the right answer, he thinks. Kai snorts at it, not quite amusement but appreciation nonetheless. He makes no move to stand up, and so Eli does not move either, only stands there, watching.

"It's not a solution, you know," Kai says, staring out across the water. "Maybe we help some dragons, but that's not the real problem. We're just treating the symptoms. Breeders who care more about profit than the actual health of their dragons, owners who'd rather throw out their pets than deal with the work of rehoming them, the fact that the world keeps getting warmer but companies are still dumping chemicals in rivers and drilling holes for oil and the government doesn't care — we can't treat that. Whatever we do, it's a temporary fix, a fucking band-aid on a stab wound."

"It's a start."

"It's not enough."

"It's not," Eli agrees. "But it's something."

A world away, a woman tugs at her boyfriend's arm, coaxing him toward a family of ducks bobbing in the lake. Plump-cheeked children dart ahead of their parents in a makeshift game of tag, leaving a whirlwind of popsicle sticks and wrappers in their wake. Eli can hear the distant but rising swell of music signaling the beginning of Dr. Wang's play. The cowherd and the weaver girl about to sweetly meet once again, unaware of the star-crossed tragedy awaiting them.

"Come on," Eli says, putting a hand on Kai's shoulder. Eli can feel the sharp edge of bone, the heat of Kai's skin through his thin T-shirt. "We should see the rest of the festival."

Kai doesn't respond for a moment, and then he shakes his head. "I can't do this," he says. "I'm sorry, but — you should go back, but I'm not ... I can't be here anymore."

There are a hundred things Eli wants to do, a million things he wishes he could say as he watches Kai, shoulders hunched and shadows under his eyes like permanent bruises. Knees hugged to his chest like a child, curled in on himself in an expression of the old, preconscious instinct that compactness equates safety.

"All right," Eli says. "Let's go."

The route to Kai's apartment is familiar, but the trains are crowded at this hour of the evening, so they walk most of the way. It's a good night, the heat present but not oppressive for once. Past the busy main streets the side roads are empty, without children playing or families holding court outside. Kai is grateful for that. He's grateful for many things: the relative coolness of the day, the dimness of the streets they are on, the distance from the Summer Palace with all its gold-gilt ostentation and crowds, and the way the stillness of his current environment, rundown though it is, nonetheless helps him breathe again. The fact that though Eli has seen Kai petty and confrontational and fending off an irrational panic attack in a public park, Eli says nothing, walks beside him without commenting or expressing concern.

Kai knows, when he sneaks a glance at Eli's face, the serenity there is genuine — Eli is a terrible liar, even more so when he's upset. But, as always, Kai has to wonder where that calm comes from. How, after all this, Eli is still here.

"Sorry I kept you from the festival," Kai says. Someone's used mattress leans against a wall, cockroaches scuttling in and out of torn fabric and exposed coils. "If you wanted to — if there was anything you wanted to see, you should go back. I can find my way to my apartment by myself."

"It's all right," Eli says, and his smile, as always, is kind. "There wasn't anything I wanted to do, anyway."

That's not the point, Kai thinks. He focuses on the slowed pulse of the city around them, the rare breeze in the air, the warmth of Eli close by if not quite touching.

"I know it's not perfect," Eli says after a while, eyes following the winking lights of an airplane in the in the sky as they walk on, "but it's a good thing you're doing. You'll be taking dragons from the streets, and they'll be getting proper medical care, maybe even homes later, if any of the students want to keep them. Because of you, Kai. You're doing something good."

"Right," Kai says, shoulders involuntarily hunching as he frowns at the ground. "One thing. In a city where thousands of people starve each day."

"It's more than what most are doing."

Under the glow of the streetlights, moths drift slowly upwards, floating motes of dust pulling inexorably toward the light.

Kai pauses to arrange his words. "It's not that I don't — I do appreciate it, everything you've done. Your professor didn't have to do anything, didn't have to hear us out at all. It is doing good, I know. But I've been doing this for so long by myself, and to have all this happen now, it just feels ..."

"It's all right," Eli says. He places a hand on Kai's back, tentative but warm. "I know. I don't mind."

You should, Kai thinks. What does it say about him that his reaction to good news is to wonder what it means for him, what it says about him and everything he's been trying to accomplish? All those months scavenging supplies and eating instant noodles so he could buy bandages, those late nights spent covered in saltwater and blood as he tried to coax

116

dangerously dry shuilong back to life — what does any of that mean, if help was always so close and so easy? How much more could he have done if he hadn't been so stubbornly self-sufficient, if he hadn't needed a project to anchor him in the face of uncertainty? How self-centered is he to wonder about this now, when there are so many more objectively important things he should be doing to prepare for what comes next?

What comes next?

What is he going to do once the work is over, when it is just him and the future in all its yawning emptiness? For all its fatality, shaolong progresses gradually. Will the rest of his life be another five years of this, whiling away the days alone? Awaiting the inevitable?

Above them, the clouds darken.

"Sorry," Kai says. There are cracks in the pavement, and he traces their patterns, the way the lines spider and expand through grey asphalt. "I should have warned you when we met. I'm not very good company." It's important that he apologize for this now, when the impulse to do it is still bright in his mind.

Eli's smile is teasing, "I've known that for a while now, thanks."

To the rude gesture Kai offers in response, Eli, the bastard, only laughs.

The silence, when it settles again, is a comfortable one. In the distance, a car alarm screeches to life, going off once, twice before stopping; above them, perched on telephone wires and rusted rooftops, cicadas buzz a slow, steady drone in the summer heat. In one of the apartments above them, a couple is fighting, raised voices audible even from the ground. The arguing figures are silhouettes behind a curtained square of light, puppet people acting out a shadow play. One figure — a man, Kai guesses from the silhouette's height and the baritone pitch of the voice — raises his hands in the air, exasperated. The other figure, smaller and more feminine looking, leans forward until her face is nearly touching the man's. Muffled accusations, agitated movements; glass breaks loudly enough that the couple pauses, pulling away as if realizing for the first time that their fight is being broadcast to the street below. The figures move into the apartment, shadows pulling themselves from the windows until all that is left is the white drapery, fluttering in the breeze of an unseen fan.

"Well," Kai says, as the voices fade away, argument muted but no doubt still simmering, "that's something I'm sure you'll miss when you're in America."

"Oh, I don't know," Eli says as he continues studying the apartment above them. "Boston in the middle of winter, I'm sure you could find similar scenes."

"As bad as this though?"

"As bad as this," Eli confirms, stepping forward so that their arms touch, the slightest hint of contact. "You know," he says, fingers tentatively curling around Kai's, "I don't think America's as great as you think. Poverty, inequality, police brutality, political incompetence, and apathy to it all — we've got the same problems there. Maybe not the same way you do, but people have a gift for being shitty no matter where they are. The US likes to make a big deal of how much more 'democratic' and 'free' it is, but when you look at what their governments actually do, America and China aren't all that different." There's a quiet acceptance to Eli's words that makes Kai feel suddenly guilty, aware of the unconscious myopia that has colored Kai's interactions with him.

"I know," Kai says, choosing his words with care. "I mean, I know that logically. People are always people, regardless of where they are. I read the news; intellectually, I know that the America you see in movies is the story it likes to tell itself, not the way it actually treats people who don't fit its definition of 'American,' whether those people are foreigners or if they've lived there all their lives. But I've never been to America. Only China, and I can see what's wrong here."

"What if you could, though?"

"I'm sorry?"

"Visit America," Eli says, kicking at something on the ground. "I know the process isn't easy, but it's not the moon, either — people go there all the time. And like I told you, my mom's a lawyer, she'd know how to get you through the process. A lot of schools do semester or year abroad programs, and my mom's has welcomed international students before. She knows about scholarships and what colleges want to see on applications. There might be some administrative issues with transferring credits and financial aid, but it's not like you're applying for a fellowship. Half my dorm did study abroad, and I don't think their reasoning went far beyond 'Paris is cool and I'd like to do cool things there.' With more fluff about 'forging international bonds' and 'expanding intellectual borders,' but you get the point."

Eli's tone is casual, but nothing else in his stance is. Shoulders stiff and hunched, he shifts subtly from foot to foot, studying the pavement with too much interest for indifference.

"You've been thinking about this for a while, haven't you?" The moment he says it, Kai knows it is true.

Eli shrugs, neither a denial nor agreement. "Does it matter? It's a good idea."

"Of course it matters," Kai says, and despite himself, he can feel the anger coming back, a steady, familiar heat under his skin. "Rearranging my life behind my back — I told you I don't want your pity, and I sure as fuck never wanted this, trying to make what *you* think are the best choices for *me*. For fuck's sake, Eli, I live here — my family, my friends, everyone I've ever known is in China. My mother's here, and you think I can just pick myself up and leave —"

"Can't you?" Eli asks. "It's not like she knows that much about your life."

"So you think it's better if I tell her all at once. Hello, Mom, I'm sick, gay, and in America."

"I'm not saying that," Eli says, and his frustration mounts as he drags a hand over his face.

119

Good, Kai thinks, *all the politeness, all that fucking patience finally running out.*

"But Kai, it's been months, and you still haven't told anyone, not your college or your friends or — or anyone. And I know you don't like taking help, but you know you can't go on like this forever —"

"So you're saying I should do what instead? Leave my family, go to America with you to get this help you're so insistent on offering, and for what? Another year, another few years, maybe ten if I'm lucky — but what then?"

"That'd still be something. You don't know, Kai, medicine advances so rapidly these days. You've heard Dr. Wang say it a hundred times. You haven't even *tried* — there are drugs, resources —"

"Resources that could be spent on more important things."

"You're important! Goddamn it, Kai, I can't keep watching you kill yourself!"

A dark night, an empty stadium looking out onto other empty stadiums, carapaces still plastered with peeling advertisements from 2008. Beijing spread out beneath him, but no one close enough to see if he let himself fall, another tragedy in a city full of thousands of them. Blood in his mouth and the promise of death in his lungs, a weight pressing lead-heavy on his chest and pushing out any last air —

Kai pushes the memory away. "That's not what I'm doing."

"Isn't it?" Eli's voice is gentle, even as his words refuse to be. "Cutting yourself off from the world, refusing to get any help — what else would you call that, Kai?"

"You think it's so easy," Kai says, and he can't suppress his bitterness now. "You Americans, with your self-help and therapeutic confessions — you think if you get everything out in the open, that solves it all, makes everything better because you say it out loud. All that talk about honesty, but you haven't told your mother about us either, have you?"

"That's not the same thing —"

"Isn't it?"

"*Kai*," Eli says, infuriatingly calm as his fingers close around Kai's wrist, "this isn't about me, and you know it. You can't keep walking away from this conversation —"

"Can't I?" A jerk back, pulling his arm out of Eli's reach; a sharp turn, not away but toward, so that Kai stretches to his full height and stares into Eli's eyes. "It's a conversation about me, isn't it? My life, Eli, my choice. You can't make me your pet project because you feel guilty about something that happened to someone else. It's not fair to you or me or your grandmother."

Eli reels back as if he'd been slapped. "Is that why you think I'm doing this? That I'm here because of some sense of misplaced guilt?"

Kai shrugs, forces himself to hold Eli's gaze. "Maybe not all of it, no. But in the beginning, when we first met ... what else would you call it?" It's the wrong thing to say, the wrong time and place to have this conversation, on a darkened side street with both of them at the end of their respective ropes, but Kai has never been good at either patience or tact. Kai's chest hurts, an invisible weight pressing inexorably down on his lungs. For a second, he can't breathe.

There's hardness in Eli's eyes, a flinty edge Kai has never seen before. It's unfair how even now, standing in a garbage-strewn street with anger in every line of his stance, Eli is still so gorgeous, all strong jawline and long, dark eyelashes out-lined against his face in the golden streetlights. Is this it? The tipping point, the moment Eli understands what Kai has been saying all along, that it's all too much and that he isn't worth it? Odd, then. He should feel vindicated, but all Kai can think about is how much he wants to draw Eli: sketch him in char-coal and ink and color his skin with thick rich oils, stencil the arc of Eli's cheekbones across the stars so that months from now, Kai can look up and marvel anew at the fine geometry of his face.

Eli closes his eyes, inhaling, and it is gone, his alien anger passing as abruptly as it had appeared.

"It's late," Eli says. The statement perfectly level, perfectly reasonable. "You're tired and so am I — we should be getting back. We can talk later."

"Later," Kai echoes — a promise or a goodbye, he isn't sure.

6

The glare of the fluorescent lights is reproachful as Eli makes his way through deserted hallways, the clack of his shoes against tile echoing in the emptiness of the Natural Sciences Building. It's late, the rest of his colleagues are either home or out for post-dinner drinks, but Eli doesn't mind; he likes working nights, the particular sense of silent communion that comes with being alone in a building with only lab equipment and beeping machinery for company. It's calming, the way his body falls into a familiar routine of PCR cycles and data entry as his mind floats above it, thoughts clearer in the near silence.

A few of the dragons protest when Eli turns on the lights, but most settle for blinking blearily before settling back down to sleep. It's only been a few days since Dr. Wang commandeered an underused classroom to move Kai's dragons in, but the mix of plentiful food and cooing grad student attention means they have adjusted well.

The dragon now numbered TF0006 chirps as Eli approaches, tail sweeping from side to side as he tracks Eli's progress. "Hi, Xiao Huang," Eli says, smiling as he opens the cage; with a jerky flutter of wings, Xiao Huang hops onto his gloved hand, impatient despite the bandages still covering one leg. Cabin fever most likely, and Eli doesn't blame him — according to Kai, there were singed holes in Xiao Huang's wings when he found him scavenging the trashcans near a sprawling shao kao restaurant, delicate membrane stretched taut and near translucent between jutting bones. Whether the injuries are the result of extended exposure to barbeque smoke from the tables of restaurant patrons or simple human cruelty, bored schoolchildren burning small creatures for entertainment, Eli isn't sure he wants to know. Either way, Xiao Huang has healed extraordinarily well since, enough that Dr. Wang's grad students have furiously scribbled notes about tissue regeneration and genome sequencing to develop new protocols for rehabilitation and research from the observations. Accelerated healing or not, Xiao Huang's injuries mean it's been weeks since he last flew properly.

Distracting Xiao Huang with a piece of dried squid, Eli rummages through the supply cabinets for treats and flight equipment. Despite all the times Kai has demonstrated the process, Eli is still clumsy as he fixes the jesses on Xiao Huang's legs, but the dragon tolerates it with surprising equanimity, lifting his legs to let Eli slip each anklet on. Eli scratches beneath his chin, and Xiao Huang rumbles in approval, transparent third eyelids lazily rolling over his golden eyes.

Former house pet is Kai's hypothesis on Xiao Huang's past, his behavior speaking to positive interactions with humans and rudimentary behavior if not flight training. Eli wonders if it was abandonment, a family unable to take care of one more mouth, or if there is some little girl or boy in Beijing still searching the skies for their lost pet.

Kai would say it doesn't matter, that it's been long enough that any bereaved owners would have lost hope. That it's useless to lose sleep worrying about it. Kai would say this because it is the pragmatic way to think. For all that Kai is fundamentally kind — a description he would no doubt laugh at — Kai likes to think of himself as practical. No room for speculative *what-ifs* or regret; there's too much to be done and no time for futile sorrow.

But Kai is not here.

A few students glance curiously at Eli as he walks toward the empty soccer pitch with a dragon on his arm, but it's late enough that most passersby are focused on making their way home. Xiao Huang is off like a shot the second Eli releases his jesses, the thin creance line tethering him to Eli like a balloon string around a child's wrist.

At first, Eli watches him carefully, but when Xiao Huang seems content with flying lazy circles around the field, Eli relaxes his grip on the line and takes out his phone. A few new emails, most of them administrative or promotions; a picture from Tycho sent to the exchange student group chat, a blurry selfie of him and Evangeline throwing peace signs outside a karaoke bar.

Nothing from Kai. But Eli isn't expecting anything.

It's been a week of intermittent texts and stilted hellos, paths inevitably intersecting despite their mutual unease. Dr. Wang had enlisted Eli in transporting the dragons from Kai's apartment to Beida, and Kai's been around the lab, explaining the personality quirks of each dragon and helping develop care plans for each one. Outside of avoiding Eli, Kai is the picture of professional helpfulness at Beida, unerringly polite as he answers researchers' questions. But Eli watches the subtle slump of his shoulders when Kai thinks no one is watching, and he fights the urge to ask Kai whether he's been sleeping, if he's been remembering to take care of himself in between all his Good Samaritanism.

It won't be welcome, and more than that, Eli isn't sure if he's ready to close the distance between them yet. They've both apologized, admitted wrong, and promised forgiveness for hurt mutually delivered, but that doesn't mean they're ready to talk.

Pet project. Even now, days later and forgiveness honestly delivered, the words still burn. The idea that after all this time, Kai would think that Eli is acting out of pity — that isn't how he looks at it, how he ever looked at Kai. His grandmother died from shaolong, yes, but that doesn't mean anything except that Eli has a better understanding of the disease and a stronger stake in his research. It certainly doesn't mean he's doing this out of guilt, of all fucking things. Yes, there are similarities between his grandmother's situation and Kai's, but being aware of those parallels doesn't mean his feelings for Kai are nothing but Freudian projection. It's simple human empathy, seeing your own experiences reflected in someone else's pain and wanting to help.

But you weren't the one who was sick, a voice reminds him. That was your grandmother, and in the end, she chose —

Footsteps sound behind him, and Eli turns to see Mr. Lin, a tianlong the size of a large owl perched on each shoulder. Unlike Xiao Huang, these dragons have only thin bands and bells around their legs, but Mr. Lin has far more experience with dragons than Eli does.

Mr. Lin raises a hand, a silent greeting that Eli mirrors. Xiao Huang glides down, wings snapping shut as he lands on Eli's glove. Eli raises his arm so that Xiao Huang can sniff at the dragons on Mr. Lin's shoulders, who tolerate the greeting with aristocratic politeness. Mr. Lin rolls his eyes, reaching out to pet Xiao Huang's neck. He clicks his tongue, and the two dragons are gliding up and off into the air, midnight blue wings almost invisible against the night sky.

"So," Mr. Lin says as Xiao Huang races to join them, determined despite having a third the wing span of the other dragons. "You two still on that lover's spat, or what?"

"I'm sorry?"

"You and Kai," Mr. Lin says, pulling some dried fish out of a plastic sandwich bag. He whistles, catching the attention of the dragons before he tosses a handful of anchovies into air; the tianlong dive, a blur of dark blue scales snatching scraps from the air. Slower than the larger dragons, Xiao Huang hovers around Mr. Lin, chirping piteously until he relents and digs out another piece of fish for him.

"What?" Mr. Lin says, raising an eyebrow when he turns to Eli. "You think just because I'm old I'm blind too?"

"I — how long have you known?"

"A while. Not that I care either way, but you two aren't as subtle as you think." Mr. Lin rolls his neck back and forth, uninterested in Eli's imminent death by mortification. His eyes are fixed on the dragons, flying lazy loops above them.

"You know that Kai's sick too?" Eli says once he trusts himself to speak again.

"Yeah." Mr. Lin takes a lighter out, cupping a hand around the flame as he lights a cigarette. "Kid doesn't let it show much, but it's not that hard to tell, once you know what to look for. You'd know that, wouldn't you?" His eyes flicker over to Eli, but his gaze is sharp. Eli can't help wondering what else Mr. Lin has figured out, how many of the secrets Eli's been holding so close have been painfully transparent all along.

"I keep trying," Eli finally says. "Telling him that he should see a doctor, get some proper treatment. But he — he won't take help. Every time I bring it up, he just shuts down, and I — it's a lot. He's getting worse, but he won't listen."

"And you think I'd know how to get through to him, knowing him longer?"

"Well, not exactly," Eli says, watching as Xiao Huang dives at one of the tianlong, who barely deigns to acknowledge him, "but I was hoping you might have some tips."

Mr. Lin barks out a laugh. "If only! Kai doesn't listen to me half the time, and I pay him — kid's a fucking enigma, and that's when he's not busy being a pain in the ass. My advice, do whatever it is you've been doing, and don't put up with too much of his bullshit. The rest of it's on him. *Teachers open the door, but you must enter by yourself.* Old Chinese saying, by the way. Free of charge, though you'll have to pay for a full explanation."

"I've been taking Chinese since I was five; I know what it means."

"See?" Mr. Lin says, flashing Eli a sharp grin. "No bullshit, just like that." He exhales, a long plume of smoke hovering briefly in front of them before dissipating into the night air. "Way I see it, you're already doing better than most people would."

Chaoyang at night is not all that different from Chaoyang in daylight: bright, loud, and crowded with enough rich expats to fund a small country's GDP. Most days, Kai finds the district exhausting, too much noise and light and conspicuous consumption, but on nights like this, he is drawn to the hum of Beijing's glittering streets, the oversaturation of stimuli a soothing respite from his own mind.

Yuye House is a small, unpretentious bar identical to any other dive bar across China if not for its queer clientele, though that crowd is here less as a result of branding than convenience. Close enough to Sanlitun for the rich foreign crowd to spill over, the bar is also far enough and dim enough for the escorts and rent boys to feel safe plying their trade. By the doorway, where a small phalanx of fans struggles valiantly against the heat, three men are engrossed in a game of twenty-four, poker-faced as they slap down cards. In a back corner, two boys sit together, legs entwined as they share swigs from a bottle of Shaanxi guopi — Kai can't tell their age, but they can't be out of high school. One of the boys leans his head against the other's shoulder, smiling at him with such open adoration that Kai feels like he's intruding. Another round of shared swigs, a lingering gaze, and they're kissing, slow and unworried in the smoky film noir light.

Kai turns back to his beer. There's condensation dewing up on his mug, and he drags a finger through it, idly tracing flowers through the cool glass.

He knows, more than anything, that this isn't sustainable. Skipping work, avoiding Eli — short of leaving the city altogether, Kai doesn't think he can evade Eli much longer. Eli is stubborn, especially when he thinks he's right. Kai can't avoid him forever. If Kai's being honest with himself, he isn't entirely sure he wants to.

If Kai tries, he can summon it up again, that familiar wave of indignation as he remembers Eli standing there in all his self-righteousness, talking about *should* and *ought to*. As if by reading about shaolong in books he automatically knows best, like Kai isn't the one with dead cilia in his lungs and throat and an immune system turning against itself, like it isn't Kai's life they're talking about. It's his life, his choice, and he could do what he wanted with it —

His mother's face flashes through his mind, that glowing smile as they read his gaokao results — happiness, yes, and pride, but no surprise. As though she had expected this all along, as though there was no other future she could have fore-seen except this, a top score and a top school for her provincial son.

For an instant, that proud smile had erased all the tired-ness from her face, leaving her as young and beautiful as in his childhood memories.

Kai tips back his beer, scowling when he finds the glass empty.

That is the problem with Elijah Ahmed, has been since the start: infuriating as it may be, he's not wrong.

At least the beer here is cheap, Kai thinks as he orders another Harbin. The bartender hands him a can from the fridge behind the counter, popping open the tab as Kai counts out exact change. Back at his table, Kai pours the beer out into his glass, watching as the foam fizzes into liquid.

"Kai?" a voice calls, startling him out of his thoughts. "Xiang Kaifei?"

It's Paofang. Wu Paofang with his European clothes and K-pop blue hair, Paofang whose dad works in Shenzhen and who wears his sexuality with the confidence of the effortlessly rich. Except this isn't Destination or Red Dog, this is a dusty dive bar populated by locals and off-hours escorts looking for a place to unwind with their makeup off.

But there's no time to wonder about any of that, because Paofang is walking toward him, a drink in his hand and a smile on his face.

"Hey, Kai! I thought it was you, but it's so dark here —"

"Hi, Pao," he says, trying for nonchalance. "Didn't expect to see you either."

"You're telling me," Paofang says, grinning as he settles in the seat next to him. "Haven't seen you since, what — April? May? Last semester, definitely. Where'd you disappear to, last few weeks of school? I know finals are always weird, but you vanished — no texts, no calls, nothing. We all wondered what happened."

"Things got busy, that's all. Essays and finals, and then I had to go home for a while, and between that and everything else, I lost track of things, I guess." Kai assiduously studies his beer, trying not to look nervous. It's a lazy lie, but then again, he had never quite thought through what he would tell people. Had always assumed that he would be able to skip that step altogether, could simply disappear within the city.

A small part of him, the part that these days speaks in Eli's voice, asks *well, what did you expect?* Beijing is a big city, but it's not so big that he could avoid familiar faces forever, especially not when he keeps being drawn by habit to old haunts. Stupid, stupid, *stupid*. What was he thinking —

"Kai?" Pao asks, head tilted to one side. "You all right?"

"Yeah," Kai says, reaching for his beer. He takes a long gulp, letting the motion soothe him. "Sorry, just distracted. Think I might have had a few too many."

Pao studies him. Standing in a dimly lit bar in an *Iron Man* T-shirt with his piercings reduced to a few small studs, he looks startlingly normal, like any other college classmate instead of the prospective heir of a successful shipping company. At Beishida, their paths might have crossed, the inevitable consequence of being tongzhi within an extremely insular community, but they had been friendly acquaintances, not friends. Paofang is rich and charming, and Kai has always felt a distance from him, one he assumed that Pao would never be interested in crossing.

"You should have told us you were in town," Pao says, smiling with his megawatt idol smile, the one that makes legions of straight girls lament their misfortune. "Campus is basically empty these days, but enough of our crowd's still around that we could have done something. Jing Hu was helping organize a photography exhibit a while back, something about dating apps and modern-day relationships. Honestly, I couldn't understand half of what she was saying but it sounded like something you art types get excited about. We can still go, if you're interested." A hand on his forearm, more perfunctory flirtation than anything; Pao has a partner, and even if they aren't exclusive, Kai's seen the types of men Pao picks up, all tan muscle and advertisement-perfect blonde hair.

"Excuse me," Kai says, standing up and pulling out his phone, making a show of assiduously studying the screen. There's a tightness in his chest, and his heart is rabbit-quick. Is it the alcohol? He hasn't had that much to drink, has he? "I think there's something I need to do."

It's a transparent excuse, but Kai can't do this anymore. They're not friends, and he won't let Pao offer companionship out of some misplaced sense of altruism, won't be someone's pity fuck.

"Ah," Pao says, disappointment evident even as he tries to hide it behind a smile. "See you around sometime, yeah?"

Kai nods, not looking him in the eyes.

Lying on his bed, pillows stacked behind him and bedside lamp dimmed, Eli opens his laptop. On the screen, his mother's Skype avatar stares back at him, small green dot at the bottom of the photo declaring her *Active*.

131

Eli knows he doesn't have to do this. Despite what Kai may have said, Eli doesn't tell his mother everything — doesn't feel the need to and has never felt like their relationship has suffered because of it. This thing between Kai and him, whatever it is and whatever it says about him — Eli knows that he does not owe it to anyone to disclose his sexuality, whatever he thinks it may be.

He wants to, though. For all their clashes, his mother has always been the person he trusts most, the person he's turned to whenever he's had a problem he couldn't solve on his own. Perhaps not the smartest person he knows — that is, and has always been, his father — but close, and steadier by far than his father has ever been.

He knows that, logically, he has little to fear. Boston University is a liberal university; plenty of his mother's colleagues are out, and she's taught queer students before, mentored them and invited them for Thanksgiving dinner. But it's different when it's your own child. His mother has cousins, but no siblings, has always implicitly imagined a future for him with picket fences and child-friendly minivans, a nice girl with in-laws enough to make up for the family she didn't have. In Massachusetts, perhaps that kind of life that could be imagined with *nice boy* in place of *girl*, but not when *boy* comes attached to *average prognosis of three to seven years*.

And Eli knows too, when he lets himself dwell on it, that if this is so hard for him, it must be a thousand times worse for Kai. Kai, who is living this diagnosis instead of merely recounting it; Kai, who is gay in a country where that fact is only starting to be admissible. Kai, who loves his mother so fiercely he would carve out pieces of himself in the name of protecting her.

Eli closes his eyes, takes a deep, shuddering breath, and clicks *call*.

"Eli, hello!" His mother, in a pixelation now familiar, smiles at him. "How are you? You said you wanted to ask me something?"

"Hey, Mom," Eli says, settling against his pillows. "Did you decide on what to get for the baby shower?"

"I'm leaning toward a mix of small things, some clothes and maybe one of those slings. Don't try to distract me, though — you know that doesn't work on me. What did you want to talk to me about?"

"Such a lawyer," Eli sighs. His mother shrugs, unrepentant. Well then. No getting around it now.

"Mom?" he asks, smoothing the blanket on his lap. "Do you remember the friend I talked about before?"

"The one you were trying to help? Did something happen, Eli? Is everything okay?"

"No," he says, shaking his head, "it's not that — nothing's changed. It's just — when I said he was my friend, I wasn't being completely honest. I mean, we are friends — I think we still are, at least. But when I said friend, I didn't mean just as a friend, but as — as ... a boyfriend."

They haven't discussed labels, and Eli has a suspicion that Kai isn't the type for such sentimentally sticky terms as 'boyfriend.' But it's the closest term he can think of right now, the clearest and most concise way to sum up these feelings — attraction, affection, mingled exasperation and apprehension — between them. And it is important, telling the first person besides Kai for the first time, to be as clear as possible.

Part of Eli wants to close his eyes, avoid the moment the realization sinks in, but he doesn't. Can't. His gaze is glued to his mother's face and every minute flicker of expression there.

Seven thousand miles away, his mother sighs, adjusts her position in her seat. "Oh, Eli. Sweetheart. Baobei." One hand reaches forward, stroking the screen. "What's his name?"

Eli swallows, the lump rising unexpected in his throat. "Kai. Xiang Kaifei."

"And he's a nice boy, Kai?"

"Not really? He's stubborn and sarcastic, and sometimes he's a confrontational asshole just for the sake of it — idiot tried to fight a street vendor because he was selling dragon skin. It wasn't even real and Kai's maybe one hundred and fifteen pounds, but he was ready to hit him for it. He's not nice, but ... he's good, Mom. Grandma would have liked him."

His mother smiles. It is her mothering smile, the same expression Eli remembers from a childhood's worth of grazed knees and formless nightmare fears: soft as blankets, warm as the honeyed milk his mother made for sleepless nights. "I'm sure she would, Eli. I'm sure your dad and I will too, if you decide to introduce him to us. Was that what you were so worried about, baobei? That I wouldn't approve because he's a boy?"

"That's part of it, but not all of it." Eli sighs, rubbing the heel of a hand over his eyes. "He's sick, Mom. He has shaolong, and he's not getting help, and I keep trying to get him to do something, but he won't listen. He doesn't think there's anything he can do. I mean, I get it. It's his life, and I can't barge in and force him to do what I think is right — and even if I did, who knows how much it would fix anyway?" Eli swallows, forces himself to breathe. "I'm not naïve. I know the treatments are still incredibly basic, won't cure him or maybe even do anything at all. But I can't watch him do nothing. I can't do that again."

Eli remembers his grandmother's gaunt face on a phone screen, serene as she asked about his classes, extracting a promise from him to visit soon, maybe that summer if he could. He remembers the glare of his computer screen at 3:00 a.m. as he scoured medical articles and forum discussions, searching for something, anything that might help when both the Western and traditional medicine had stopped working. Then, finally, the small box mailed to his dorm room, books and photos and his grandfather's old pocket watch, mementos and trinkets bundled together *to my dearest grandson* —

"Do you know," his mother says, choosing her words carefully, "when your grandmother first told me she was going to stay in Beijing, I was furious. We tried not to do it too much around you, but we used to argue a lot, your grandmother and me. It started when I was a teenager, but we never quite stopped after that. So when she told me that no, she wasn't coming back to America, it felt a little like that — like I was seventeen again and too young to understand how the world worked."

She shrugs and smiles, half rueful, half nostalgic. "Feeling like that, I reacted a little like a teenager would. I regret that now. I still don't know if I should have pushed harder to get her to leave Beijing, but I regret not being kinder. Your grandmother was old, and the disease was advanced when she got the diagnosis. If she didn't want to spend her last months in waiting rooms and doctor's offices — well, I should have tried to understand that."

"It's not the same though. Kai's my age, and he isn't — it isn't that far, with him. There's still time."

On screen, his mother taps her fingers against one cheek as she thinks. "You said that he won't get help. Do you know why that is?"

"Because he's a stubborn, self-destructive fuck?" Eli asks, before remembering who he's speaking to. "Sorry, Mom, but it's true. He hasn't even told his family because he thinks they don't need to know, because his mom's not going to worry when he drops off the map for months on end? And Kai's not stupid, not usually at least, but every time I try to bring it up, he gets so stubborn. We got into a fight about it last week, and we haven't talked since. Really talked I mean, not awkward small talk and hellos when we see each other. If it's going to be the same arguments over and over again, then I ..."

"Then it's hard to know if you want to keep on trying," she finishes. "If it's worth it, when nothing seems to change. I know, baobei. I know."

Knees pulled to his chest, Eli nods. "I don't know what to do. If I can do anything that would help."

"You're helping now though. With the research you're doing right now and the fact that you so obviously care about him. I think you've been doing more than you give yourself credit for."

"But it's not enough. Not if nothing's going to change and Kai will still — if it's not going to help, then it's not enough."

"No," his mother says. "But that's the way with anything worth doing, isn't it? You work and work, and there's always a risk of whether it's enough or not, of whether any of this is going to make any difference or if it's just months sunk into another hopeless case. But you do the work. Because it's what you can do. Because you may never know if it means anything, but on the chance that it does, you can't live with yourself if you don't try, can you?"

Long seconds pass, the only noise between them the whir of computers and the almost inaudible sound of ragged breathing.

His mother's lips are pursed when Eli finally collects himself enough to look up again. "Eli," she begins, then stops. She looks like she wants to say something, but then she exhales — a long, steady breath — and gives him her softest smile. "Take care of yourself, okay?"

Eli nods, trying to smile even as he wipes his eyes. "Yeah. I will. Thanks, Mom."

The ceiling is blurry when Kai wakes up, sheets sweat-sodden and head pounding with the percussive force of a brass band. His throat feels like it's been scraped with sandpaper. He aches, a full-body bruise feeling Kai recognizes as the telltale sign of a fever.

"*Fuck*," Kai moans, covering his face with his hands. Even that movement hurts, pain a sharp spike flashing behind his eyes. Hungover and sick — of course. Just his luck.

From her place atop the bedframe, Mei leans down to nose at his hair. "Shh," Kai tells her. "It's okay, it's all right. Go back to sleep, baobei." Mei grumbles but lowers her head, wings shifting as she curls into the shape of a cozy baozi.

Eyes closed, Kai tries to wait out the pain and fall back to sleep. But his head throbs and the sunlight filtering through the window is unrelentingly bright. He's still dressed in his clothes from last night, sweat and grime clinging to his sheets and his skin.

His body protests as he forces himself out of bed, but Kai manages to stumble to the bathroom somehow. He stands in front of the mirror, propping himself against the sink as he waits for his breathing to slow.

Halfway through brushing his teeth, Kai hits some over-sensitive part of his mouth and starts coughing, a fit that sends his toothbrush clattering to the tile, stomach lurching into his throat as he struggles for breath. It takes a while, but it passes, leaving Kai with nothing worse than tear-blurred vision and a throat so raw it hurts to breathe.

Nothing too out of the ordinary then.

It would be easier, Kai thinks bitterly as he spits blood into the sink, if he followed Eli's advice and got actual treatment instead of subsisting on aspirin and hope. But that would mean seeing a doctor — would mean going to a hospital and letting them put his name and identification number into a database, irrevocably tying him to this diagnosis. Making it all, in some crucial way, inescapable. Real.

Eli thinks he is stubborn and self-destructive, a self-righteous idiot willingly walking toward martyrdom. Kai knows better. People have always seen the anger and combat-iveness and thought *bravery*, but that is only a portion of the truth. Kai has no trouble confronting bullies or calling out cruelty, has been doing so since he was a child. But he has fears, the same as everyone else.

Something cool nudges at his hand. When Kai looks down, Mei is perched at the edge of the sink, head tilted to one side as she stares at him, pupils so thin her eyes are almost pure gold. Kai sighs and lifts her onto his shoulder, murmuring apologies for worrying her as he wills his hands to stop shaking and his heartbeat to calm.

Staring at his reflection in the mirror, a splotchy stranger with hollow cheeks and red-rimmed eyes, Kai can't imagine why Pao — why anyone — would want him.

He has enough sense and energy to fill up a water bottle and knock back an aspirin before sinking face-first onto his bed, a pillow pulled over his aching head to muffle the pain as Mei carefully licks at his face. The pillow doesn't help much, but it's the illusion of control — of doing something to manage the damage — that he's after.

The route to Kai's apartment is a litany of streets and side alleys Eli could navigate in his sleep. Eli steps off the train, and then muscle memory takes over until he's sprinting up flights of creaky stairs.

"What," Kai says, struggling groggily to sit up in bed as Eli enters, "why are you — how did you get in?"

"Spare key," Eli says, trading his sneakers for house slippers. He's winded from sprinting up the stairs, but the adrenaline keeps him rushing forward. "Not that I needed it; you left the door unlocked. Mr. Lin said you texted him that you were sick, and he told me to make sure you were still alive." Pulling a chair over, Eli places a palm on Kai's forehead, marveling at how steady his hands are. From her place beside Kai's pillow, Mei slits open one eye, then closes it again. "Fuck, you're burning up."

"I normally am. It's a side effect of chronic disease."

"God, you're insufferable, you know that?" Even so, there's a part of Eli that's heartened by it — if Kai has energy to snark, he can't be that ill. Still, shaolong makes gauging that tricky, the variable of innately elevated body temperature playing havoc with what constitutes dangerous. "Your medical supplies are in the top left shelf, right?"

"Yeah," Kai sighs, seeming to accept defeat as he sags back into his pillows. "I might be out of medicine, though. Human medicine, I mean."

"Of course you are," Eli says, under his breath. The upper shelves in Kai's kitchenette are a mess of bandages and tank parts, but there's a thermometer in the meagre first aid kit in the back.

39.2°C — high but not yet dangerous for a normal patient, so probably a mid-grade fever for someone with shaolong. A quick search proves his hypothesis right, and Eli can't help the tidal wave of relief that washes over him as he skims the results. A normal cold, nothing more. Nothing to worry about. And even if autoimmune diseases made sickness difficult, turning simple fevers serious in the split-second of a blink, that's no reason to assume —

No, Eli thinks, interrupting that train of thought. Not the time for those worries and worst-case scenarios.

"Stay here," Eli tells Kai as he stands up, double-checking that his wallet is in his pocket. Kai glares in response, but it's half-hearted.

The nearest corner store pharmacy is a few minutes away, and Eli has to remind himself that it's okay, it's only a cold. Kai had been fine when he left and would be fine when he returned. Was fine, would be fine, will be fine.

He gets a selection of basic cold medicine — ibuprofen, tea and other liquids, the awful but effective throat lozenges he remembers hating as a child — before all but sprinting out of the store, the teenaged cashier barely glancing up from his phone through the entire interaction.

Kai is still in bed, scowling at the ceiling like it personally wronged him. It's irrational, but Eli can't help the wave of relief that floods him.

"Here," Eli says, placing the ibuprofen and a bottle of tea on the chair next to Kai. "Two pills every four to six hours, with water or tea. I bought some juice and other drinks, but I'm going to leave those in the fridge. You're going to want to hydrate in general, though you should try to eat if you can. Speaking of which, I doubt you've eaten anything today, so I'm going to make some congee, okay?"

Kai frowns at the items on the chair. "You don't need to look after me." He averts his eyes as he props himself up on his elbows. "I've gotten sick before. I know how to take care of myself."

"I'm bored and I don't have anything else planned right now," Eli says, deliberately light. "You're a perfect distraction. Drink your tea."

"What are you, my mother?"

"Someone needs to be," Eli says, "and if you won't let yours do her job, I might as well fill in." The words are sharper than he intends and he regrets them immediately, but he doesn't apologize. Won't, not when there are three types of dragon food in the kitchen but barely more than a half-carton of eggs in the fridge.

This time, it is Kai who looks away first. The guilt intensifies, a sharp, cold stab through Eli's chest.

He won't apologize for it. It hurts, hurting Kai, but there is only so long anyone can walk on eggshells before something breaks, and Eli is tired. Has been tired, he's realizing, for a long time.

There's a bag of rice, half-full, in the pantry cupboard. Eli busies himself with it: measuring out the rice, rinsing the grains under water, watching the dust rise to the surface, a thin film of white that dips and swirls with the jostling of the water.

Out of the corner of his eye, Eli watches Kai drink his tea. Sitting in bed in a too-big T-shirt and Mei dozing curled into the crook of his neck, Kai looks so young, a silhouette sharp and stark in the sunlight pouring into the room.

Eli looks away. Concentrates on chopping up the wilted green onion he'd found in the fridge before rummaging around Kai's cabinets, where he manages to unearth a packet of zha cai and a half-empty bottle of Lao Gan Ma sauce. It isn't much, but it will make the congee a little less plain.

Eli cares for Kai — loves him, maybe, if he lets himself think that word, if it is not too early and melodramatic to think it. He wants to help. He won't stop trying to help. But he's starting to think they're right, his mother and Mr. Lin and even Kai, damn the irony of it all. Kai isn't his personal project, and Eli can't — won't — treat him like one, some tabula rasa on which Eli can put his displaced guilt to rest.

But that doesn't mean he can't care.

On the stove, the water boils. Eli adds the rice and green onion and salt to taste, turning the heat to a simmer before replacing the lid on the pot. Nothing to do now but wait.

"Here," Eli says, sitting down by Kai and opening up his laptop. "Do you want to watch something while it cooks?"

In the silver stillness of predawn, Kai sits at the kitchen table, hands cupped around a mug of tea. Beside him, Mei perches on the windowsill, nose pressed against the glass as she surveys the awakening world outside. Though she stays silent, her tail betrays her, swishing as she watches pigeons rummage through overturned garbage.

A piece of notebook paper lies on the table, words scrawled in Eli's familiar chicken scratch. *Morning labs — sorry I can't stay, will try to stop by tonight. If you need anything, call me.* The last two words underlined twice, as if Eli is trying to impress the importance of the message on him through sheer emphasis. In spite of himself, the too-early hour, and the lingering aches, Kai smiles at it.

In Eli's wake, the floors have been swept and the counters are all but sparkling, all the dirty dishes scrubbed and dried and neatly put away. There's fresh water in Mei's tank, fresh fruit and tofu in his fridge, and packages of ice pops and dumplings in the freezer. Kai had tried to refuse the groceries, but Eli had given him a look so flatly unimpressed that Kai's teeth had clacked together as he shut his mouth. Perhaps it was the fever or the relief of seeing Eli after so many days of détente, but Kai had not wanted to do anything to risk the fragile peace between them.

By all rights, he should have been furious — the presumption with which Eli had barged in, all unwanted good intentions and *doctor's orders* high-handedness. Eli had been overbearing, but he had also brought Kai tea and made congee, kept him company even when Kai drifted off between episodes of American reality TV. For a few brief hours, it had been like a scene from childhood, staying home from school with a thermometer in his mouth and cartoons on TV as his mother made him soup and fussed over his temperature.

It's been a long time since Kai has spoken to his mother. Longer still since he last did so honestly, no secrets or pretense between them — not since his father's death, maybe. Kai doesn't regret it, the time he had spent forcing away the anger and grief so the endless sadness in his mother's eyes might fade, but he wonders sometimes what their relationship could have been otherwise. One thing had rolled into another and then, with years' practice, it had practically become a habit — lying about fevers and wrapping his own scraped elbows, hiding bruises under long sleeves and black eyes with stolen foundation.

Everyone lies. He knows that; has known it since he was small and his mother pushed away her own weariness to smooth back his hair and kiss away his tears. *It's all right Kai Kai, don't worry, your dad will be okay.* Kai had been young then, but more than old enough to hear the lie. Still, it had felt necessary somehow that she say the words, maintain the illusion of normalcy even when no one believed in it. You can't live a life without lying, can't construct a society without some measure of deceit, social niceties softening bare truth with gentler *maybes*.

And yet.

Mei chirps, sitting up as a flock of tianlong perch on a telephone line outside. She's lonely, perhaps; disoriented, certainly. The apartment, never a large space, feels empty without the background noise of a dozen small creatures chattering in their cages, without the low-grade smell of salt and dirt and metallic blood.

Kai's head throbs when he stands up, but it's a faded ache, nothing he hasn't handled before, nothing a few painkillers and gritted teeth can't cure. He sits down beside Mei, reaches one hand up to stroke down her spine. Mei leans into the touch, cool scales soothing against too-warm skin.

"I know," Kai says, scratching behind her ruff. "It's weird, isn't it? Don't worry, though. There'll be plenty of new friends soon." There will be more dragons — there will always be more dragons — but now they will have another place to go, an imperfect place perhaps but one still larger and better funded than anything Kai could provide.

Outside, the tianlong flit from pole to pole, chirping greetings in the brightening sky. There's a storm front moving in, and while the other city animals are seeking shelter, the dragons are out in full force, drawn out of their sewer and alley hideaways by the scent of ozone in the air. Tianlong taste the air with their tongues or swoop down after passing moths. Green and brown and startling sky-blue, they could be images from some ancient scroll, brought to life against grey steel skies. If Kai squints, he can almost see it — a dozen tiny gods perched in neat rows and waiting for rain.

A still warm cup of tea between his hands, Kai watches the dragons and, for the first time in a long time, feels brave enough to hope.

Storm clouds gather as Eli boards the train, dark and heavy with the promise of rain. Fitting weather for the occasion, even if the mood the weather induces is more festive than funereal. Summer-browned children stream out into the streets in a parade of bright rain jackets and toy airplanes as their pale mothers cautiously peer out of doorways. *Flash floods likely*, Eli's weather app had said, a warning that apparently means nothing to Beijing's excited citizenry.

The small cemetery is busier than the last time he visited, but that's to be expected. The Zhongyuan Festival is a holiday for family and remembrance, and so it would make sense that it would be a bustling familial occasion, mothers and fathers bringing their children to pay their respects and lay down paper offerings to loved ones long gone. Against those sprawling nuclear units — mother plus father plus child plus extended family and in-laws too — the single visitors stand out, lone figures cradling bags of clementines and unlit lotus lanterns against their chests. Who have you lost, Eli wonders as he passes each person with their small bundle of grief. Why are you alone? How do you go on?

He's one these solitary ones, of course; but that doesn't stop him from wondering. Feeling compassion, not pity — the natural heartache of seeing your experience in someone else. Simple human empathy.

"Hi Grandma, I'm back," Eli says, sitting down on the grass in front of his grandmother's grave. He reaches into his backpack for hard sesame candy and incense holders.

"Mom said to get you some fake books to burn, but they were surprisingly hard to find in shops — I can buy you a paper helicopter or five different brands of paper handbags, but not one fake wuxia trilogy. I could have brought you my old copy of *Twilight*, but that's at home and I don't think you would have liked it much anyway."

Eli lays out paper flowers and tiny clementines and sweet rice wine, arranging the objects into tidy symmetry on the grave before sitting back to study his work. A neat tableau of his grandmother's favorite things.

He wonders how long it will be before he can do this again — how long before anyone will do this again for his grandmother. Outside of an older brother now frail and nearly eighty, his grandmother's family in China is in-laws and cousins multiply removed. How long, Eli wonders, before his grandmother's old students and Beijing friends stop remembering to visit, the pull of other lives drawing them out of a dead woman's orbit? When is forgetting too soon, and when is it simply moving on? Does Eli have any right to resent them, when he too is leaving?

Dry grass rustles underfoot as a shadow falls over his grandmother's gravestone. Eli doesn't need to look up to know who it is, who could have cared enough to come all the way here.

"Hi," Eli says, placing a stick of sesame candy on top of the clementines. "This is a surprise. Were you following me?"

Kai shrugs, not quite a denial. He looks better than the last time Eli saw him, face no longer fever-flushed and eyes a little brighter. "It wasn't difficult. You tend to stand out, for some reason. It was simply a matter of asking the guard and helpful passersby until I found you."

"The curse of being a foreigner in China." Eli sighs, brushing the dirt off his knees as he stands up. "What are you doing here?"

In response, Kai hands him a piece of paper, folded neatly in quarters. "You said your grandmother liked flowers, didn't you?"

Golden chrysanthemums and red peonies reveal themselves as Eli unfolds the paper, bright colors shining in the waning light.

"It's beautiful," Eli says. Kai shrugs, eyes not meeting Eli's. It's not quite an apology, but it is a peace offering, a silent attempt at repairing the distance between them without admitting fault. "Did you bring a frame with you?"

Kai shakes his head. "It's just a sketch. I can make you a proper painting later."

"I'd still like to frame it. Sketch or not, it's really good."

Kai sighs. "You're supposed to burn it. So your grandmother can have it in the afterlife."

"I know that. I've brought a lot of things to burn. This, though, I'm keeping for myself."

Kai huffs out a laugh, the ghost of a smile in his eyes. "I can't stop you, I guess."

"You can't," Eli says, tucking the paper into a pocket. "It's mine now."

Thunder rumbles, low and lazy above them.

Eli studies Kai: the bright points of red over sharp cheekbones, the choppy line of self-cut bangs, the faint scar across his forehead from a biking accident long healed. It astonishes Eli sometimes, how little time it's been. Barely a handful of weeks, and Kai feels so familiar — each scar a story, each callus and errant freckle a landmark on a topography of pale skin.

However this ends, whatever regrets come later, Eli can't imagine regretting knowing Kai.

"So, have you given it any consideration?" Eli says, picking each word as carefully as he would broken glass. "America, I mean."

"Mm." Kai crosses his arms, eyes distant as he studies the space beyond Eli's shoulder. "Haven't been able to stop thinking about it, actually. You're annoying like that sometimes, you know?"

"So I've been told. Certain people seem to like me, in spite of or because of it, I don't know."

"Very much in spite of." The corner of Kai's lip twitches, and for a moment, it is almost as if the last week hadn't happened.

"Well?" Eli asks, because for all that he wants the easy comfort between them again, he cannot leave another conversation without knowing. "America."

"I don't know," Kai says. "Maybe." He shifts from one foot to another, still not meeting Eli's eyes. "I know you said your mother is a professor, but it won't be easy. There's still paperwork and applications to consider, and even if anyplace wanted me, I'd still have to get a passport and talk to my mom, and it's just —" Kai stops, sucks in a slow, shaky breath. He's frowning, fine lines drawn between the furrow of his brows, mouth drawn up in a grimace so sharp it looks painful.

"You don't want to hurt her."

Kai nods. "My mom — when Dad died, some of my aunts were very kind, offered to take me and my sister in so she wouldn't have to worry about us. But my mother refused. Said she was grateful, but that she wouldn't do that to us, make us grow up without both parents while she was still there and could still work. I — she's been through a lot, my mom. I don't want to add to that. You know that. But —"

Eli wraps an arm around Kai's waist, pulls him in. Kai stiffens at first, but then he's slumping against him, head bowed and buried against Eli's shoulder. Gently, the way he remembers his mother stroking his hair as a child, Eli smooths Kai's hair, wind-tousled and sweat-damp. Kai must have run here, Eli thinks as he pulls him closer, hurried straight off the platform and sprinted in the direction the guard pointed him.

It's beginning to drizzle, small, faint drops falling in a fine mist. With the flash flood warning and only one flimsy umbrella between them, they should look for shelter, head toward one of the public restrooms or mausoleums nearby.

They don't. In the trees, tianlong chatter at each other as they watch the roiling clouds above; on the ground, a few humans do the same, dressed in suits and shoes completely unsuited for rain but either uncaring or too excited by the prospect of rain to take cover.

The air is soaked in petrichor, the scent of earth and rainwater and wildflowers rising out of old ground. Kai's hand is dry and too-warm in his, heartbeat the too-fast flutter of sparrow's wings against Eli's chest: *one-two one-two one-two one-two.*

Kai's arms tighten around him, a wordless affirmation: it's all right, I know, I'm sorry, I'm here. I know.

And then, with a crack and rumble of thunder echoed by a volley of cheers from all around them, the rain comes falling down.

Acknowledgments

This book has been a very long time in the making. It owes its existence to a lot of coffee, community center free Wi-Fi, and many, many wonderful people.

Thank you to my editor, Selena Middleton, and the crew at Stelliform Press for all their hard work. At the risk of presenting this book as a sad-eyed animal in a Sarah McLachlan commercial, thanks for taking a chance on this project and for helping shepherd it into a coherent narrative.

Thank you to Neelanjana Banerjee at Kaya Press for her feedback on an earlier version of this piece, and for taking the time to meet with me. Grad school can be a disconcerting, lonely time, and Kaya Press's events have given me a valuable space to talk about craft instead of Derrida and Deleuze.

Katherine Aanensen, Misha Grifka, and Elaine Yao have listened to me scream about this project from almost the beginning (and there was a lot of screaming). Thanks for providing feedback on early drafts, sharing cute animal photos, and above all proving Dr. Chuck Tingle's thesis that love is real, for all who kiss and those who don't. May we one day meet in Chicago again, preferably with pastries and without the winter cold.

Though this novel is by no account an anthropological account of contemporary China (who uses cash these days?), thanks to Ran Deng for Beijing/China checking. Thanks also to Elikem Dorbu for help with science details and to the staff of the San Diego Chinese Historical Museum for both the 2019 Dragons exhibit and their willingness to provide further resources for research. Your help is deeply appreciated, and any factual missteps lie with me.

This book began life as a short story and was consequently workshopped as one by Vu Tran and my classmates: Abinav, Willa, Megan, Kathryn, Beau, Nick, Grace, Fitz, Juan, Dennison. Thanks for your comments and for eventually convincing me out of the short story format and into something longer. Thanks also to María, who read and commented on early drafts despite half a continent of distance between us.

As a child, I would have never imagined myself writing this, but thank you to my parents for making me take Chinese classes so I could maintain some semblance of language fluency. A lot of this piece is poached from childhood memories of visits home, so thank you to both family and family friends for hosting, feeding, and entertaining us.

Lastly, thank you to Dash, a truly dragon-hearted dog.

ABOUT THE AUTHOR

Cynthia Zhang was born in Beijing, China and grew up in various college towns before landing near St. Louis, Missouri. She studied comparative literature and creative writing at the University of Chicago, and the experience was insufficiently harrowing to prevent her from pursuing PhD work at the University of Southern California. Her work has appeared in *Leading Edge*, *Coffin Bell*, *Phantom Drift*, and other venues. *After the Dragons* is her debut novel.

Author photo by Elaine Yao.

STELLIFORM PRESS

**Earth-focused fiction. Stellar stories.
Stelliform.press.**

Stelliform Press is shaping conversations about nature and our place within it. Check out our upcoming titles and articles and leave a comment or review on your favourite social media platform.